THE DEVIL AND MISS SMY

The Devil and Miss Smy

A WINIFRED SMY
MYSTERY

Michael Heath

Fara Press

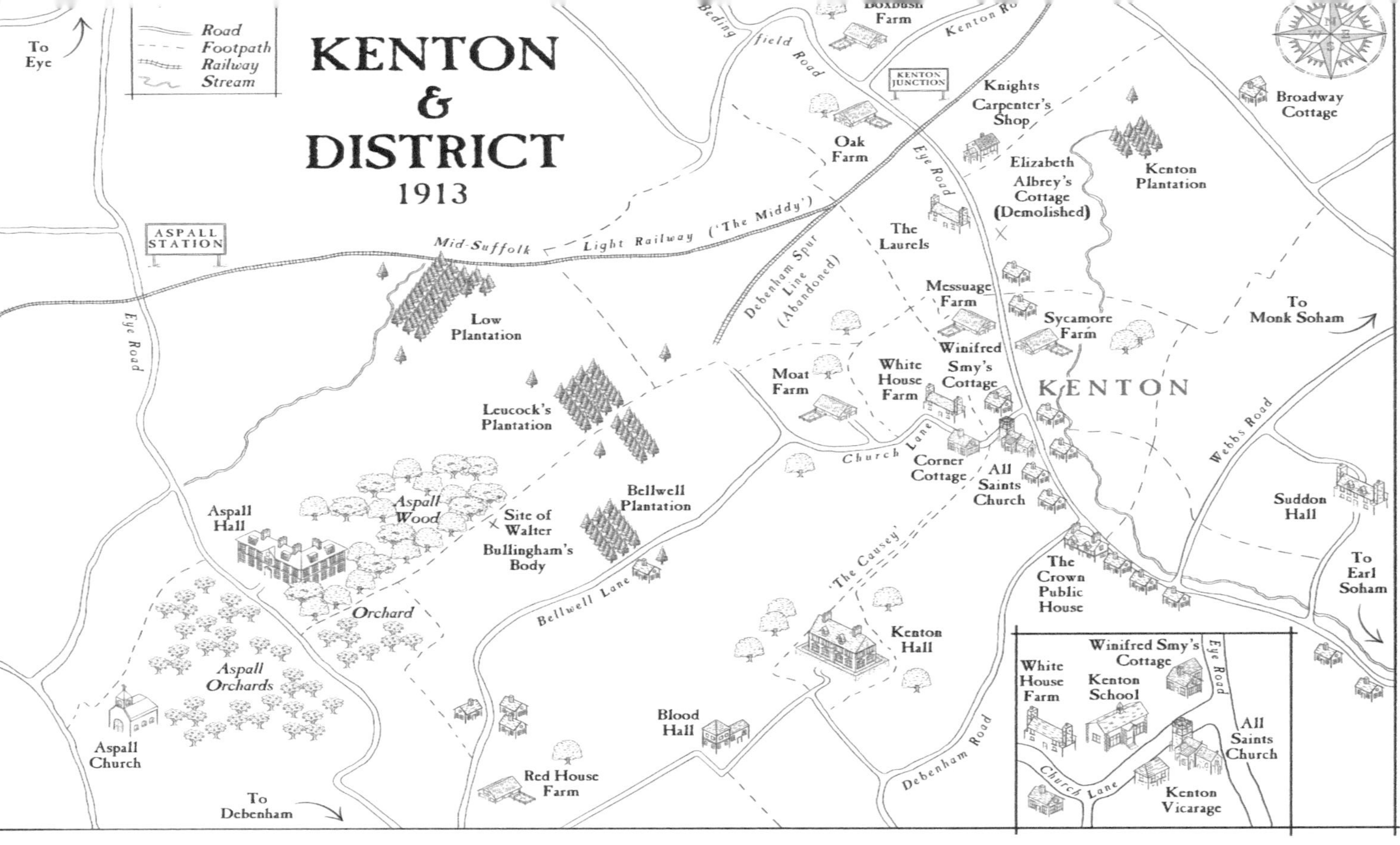

KENTON
&
DISTRICT
1913
Road
Footpath
Railway
Stream
To Eye
ASPALL STATION
Mid-Suffolk   Light Railway ('The Middy')
Eye Road
Beding field Road
BOXBUSH Farm
Kenton Rd
KENTON JUNCTION
Knights Carpenter's Shop
Oak Farm
Elizabeth Albrey's Cottage (Demolished)
Kenton Plantation
Broadway Cottage
The Laurels
Debenham Spur Line (Abandoned)
Messuage Farm
Sycamore Farm
To Monk Soham
Low Plantation
Moat Farm
White House Farm
Winifred Smy's Cottage
KENTON
Webbs Road
Leucock's Plantation
Church Lane
Corner Cottage
All Saints Church
Suddon Hall
Aspall Wood
Site of Walter Bullingham's Body
Bellwell Plantation
'The Causey'
The Crown Public House
To Earl Soham
Aspall Hall
Orchard
Bellwell Lane
Kenton Hall
Aspall Orchards
Blood Hall
Debenham Road
Aspall Church
Red House Farm
To Debenham
White House Farm
Kenton School
Winifred Smy's Cottage
Eye Road
All Saints Church
Church Lane
Kenton Vicarage

A Gobber Tooth and a Squint Eye

Harrowing cries were heard from inside the cottage that, with the flinging open of the rude front door, became immediately louder as the desperately writhing body of Elizabeth Albrey was hauled out onto the Eye Road by two men.

The small group of villagers that had gathered around watched with an excitement that was nonetheless tempered by a tacit shame. Nearby stood a well-dressed man, quite distinct from many of the others, with a self-important manner. He removed his wide-brimmed hat that bore a silver buckle at the front of the crown, raised his arm and shouted, "Hold her fast, Master Bankes!"

He slowly turned to those assembled, eyeing them as a barrister scrutinises a jury.

"Good folk of Kenton, is this your Elizabeth Albrey? The same Elizabeth Albrey to whom you wanted to direct my attention?"

Only one man answered. "That's 'er! She's the one."

"You must be Catchpole. Tell me, is this woman the one that has infected your swine with a devil's curse?"

"Why I dussant let 'em out for fear they will kill my woife or me. They've roves all over 'em and I carn't stop 'em bleeden."

"And you said your harvests have been poor, Sir?"

"Withered. Withered by that mawther's magic."

Another woman, emboldened by the exchange, added, "An' I 'eard someone says she dew sit at night with an imp on 'er lap. Talken away they said."

The man raised his eyebrow. "An imp you say. Did this person who told you mention the imp's name?"

All the villagers shook their heads.

"Come, come," the man persisted. "They often have strange, unholy names. Names that no mortal could invent: Jamara; Vinegar Tom; Holt. And they assume an evil form: polecats; black rabbits; fat spaniels. Do these not seem familiar?"

When he recognised that he would not get a response from the group, he walked over to the weeping woman, pathetic in her rags of clothes, her thin arms purpled with the violence of her restraint. As a man of short stature, he needed only to stoop slightly to look up into the face of Elizabeth Albrey.

"Is what I hear true? Do you entertain an intermediary of Satan in your very home?" He pointed at her ramshackle cottage.

But it was another voice that broke the silence. "Unhand that woman! In the name of God let her go!"

Hearing the interjection, certain villagers turned with some alarm to see the arrival of their vicar.

"Your presence is welcomed, minister," said the well-dressed man. "It will only add to the standing of those that witness the work of myself and Master Stearne." At the mention of his name, Stearne stepped forward. He was taller than many there and looked at the vicar with a cruel, unflinching eye.

"Your work is evil. You have no right to either accuse this woman or to submit her to your wicked methods."

"But she has a gobber tooth," shouted one of the villagers.

"An' a squint eye!" added another.

Hopkins walked over and stood beside the villagers. "You see, Sir, your parishioners know things you don't and see things you would rather not see. Being good Christians, they have invited myself and Master Stearne here to test if this woman is in league with Lucifer. I say to you most clearly, it is our intention to honour that commission."

"You are both nothing but charlatans, Matthew Hopkins. You have no authority. And neither does your henchman, Stearne, or these so-called 'searchers'."

Hopkins reached into a pocket and pulled a clutch of papers from it, which he held up with a dramatic flourish.

"Our authority is in these pages, Minister Geffrey; these are letters of safe conduct so that we may pursue our calling. If you do seek to question that authority, then you must do so not only with his Majesty King Charles, but with our Parliament as well."

"Those letters of safe conduct are nothing more than the endorsement of the vilest trade. You are a self-appointed madman, Hopkins. You prey on the ignorance of the poor and get handsomely rewarded for it. Even my dearest friend, John Lowes..."

"Ah, the now sadly-departed incumbent at Brandeston!" At this, Hopkins turned to the villagers. "The man your minister has brought to my attention was one who was proved to have covenanted with the devil and suckled familiars at his own breast. Good Mr Stearne, remind me of the names of those imps that Brandeston's minister nourished."

Stearne, without turning his eyes from Geffrey, coldly answered, "There was Mary, and Bess and Tom, I recall. The very cattle were bewitched by him and why if he hadn't caused a ship to sink at Harwich with his demonic influence."

"And this minister now before us is his self-confessed friend, Master Stearne. This man that casts doubt on my authority is himself a mightily troubling presence amongst us. For his coterie would seem to extend to those tried and found guilty of demonology."

The minister, a man of advanced years, walked angrily up to Hopkins but one of his assistants, Edward Parsley, stepped forward and roughly pushed him away.

"Keep him there, Mr Parsley. I have not finished with the minister quite yet. Good men and women of Kenton, we have but a short time and then must be on our way. We will take this woman that you have identified to a nearby place. My searchers, Mary Philips and Mary Parsley will need two or three of you to join them to watch over Elizabeth Albrey for a little time. If she is indeed - as you suspect - in solemn league with the devil, then we must have witnesses when she finally confesses."

"I make it clear to you," Stearne added. "We have personally been present when the foulest imps have entered the very room and run back and forth before our very eyes. We ask the searchers to look closely at this woman's body for those places where the imps do suck. Teats that hang in private places beneath her clothes."

"Will you swim her, Sir?"

Stearne turned to another of the assistants, Frances Mills. "Yes, Frances, should we need some final proof."

The minister broke free from Edward Parsley's grip and shouted with a hoarse voice, "This is against God! This is a simple woman, cursed by feebleness and age, who has done no wrong. These villagers have known her all their lives and yet suddenly accuse her of witchcraft. Catchpole's pigs are ridden with sores because he neglects them. His crops fail because he drinks himself into a stupor when he should be looking after his land."

"Enough, Minister! I have no belly for your ravings. By the grace of God, take her, Master Parsley and let the searchers commence their solemn duties. You Sir," he nodded to Catchpole. "Lead on and point out your farm."

The farmer walked ahead towards Bedingfield village, with the still struggling woman and her ghastly entourage close behind.

*　　*　　*

The Station Master of Kenton Junction, Percy Whiting, walked slowly along the platform enjoying the warmth of the

June sunshine. He removed his hat and wiped away the sweat from the inner band with a sweep of his finger. George Bloom, the fireman of the newly arrived train, stepped down and handed him a newspaper. "What yew think of that, Perce?"

Whiting brought the paper up to his chest, slid his spectacles to the bottom of his nose and slowly read out loud, "Death of Emily Davison, who stopped the King's Derby horse…" He returned the paper to Bloom with a contemptuous shake of his head. "Madness. Why are all these suffragette mawthers nan-nocking around instead of getten married, eh, George?"

"No man'll 'ave 'em, that's why. There's a place for women an' it ain't in front of no 'orses. Oh, mornen, Mrs Cupper!"

But Mrs Cupper seemed completely unaware of Percy Whiting or George Bloom. Her face was utterly without expression as if she were a mannequin blankly staring from a shop window out onto the pavement. She walked down the platform and turned on to the Eye Road towards her home. Bloom and Whiting watched her before the fireman shrugged his broad shoulders and departed with, "Best I git gorn."

Only a few minutes after this exchange, Winifred Smy stood up from the flower bed that ran along the front of her cottage, slightly arching her back to counter the stiffness she was feeling, just as Gladys Cupper was passing.

"Good morning, Gladys."

But Mrs Cupper didn't respond. The same mask-like quality of her expression remained.

"Good morning, Mrs Cupper!" repeated Miss Smy, perturbed by her neighbour's mysterious demeanour.

This time Gladys Cupper emerged with a jerk from her trance. She looked Miss Smy full in the face and slowly shook her head.

"I've seen 'im. I've seen 'im, Fred."

Miss Smy wiped her hands on her apron and walked out onto the road.

"Seen who, Glad? Who are you talking about?"

"The Witchfinder. Plain as day he was. An' he was standen by a woman. A hanging woman. Hanging she was, from a tree."

2

Will the Hunter Become the Hunted?

As the evening cloud draped itself over the weakening light, Matthew Hopkins sat meditatively on a rotted oak that had fallen in the unforgiving spring winds. He blew a final, fat ring of smoke into the evening before knocking his clay pipe on the trunk. The sound of approaching footsteps caused him to half-turn in his seat but, reassured by whom he saw approaching, he calmly resumed the cleaning of his pipe.

"Mr Stearne."

"My father said old King James thought tobacco an evil, Mr Hopkins."

"Oh, did he? Well, life must afford us small pleasures or else 'tis no life at all."

"Talking of pleasures, I hear she won't confess."

"Our Elizabeth Albrey? I was well aware of that. All I hear from yonder farm is a lot of screaming. I am afeared that our searchers are too taken with their task. They would do better to forbear some hours or so and give her time. Her imps will soon need to seek her out, I am certain."

John Stearne unbuttoned his jacket and, finding the warmth of the June evening still oppressive, began fanning himself with his hat. "She'll talk in time. We've always had the stubborn ones. You just need to find the place where they break."

"Well, she needs to break soon. We have their promise of the money. It's time we were rid of this Kenton." He looked about with quiet contempt. "Good for us to move on now, go somewhere a little bit more, shall we say, rewarding. One witch won't pay the rent, John."

An awful scream sliced across the stillness, causing Matthew Hopkins to wince with irritation. "In the name of God, if they can't bring her to her senses, then I'll be hanged if I don't bang her head against that farm wall 'til she does."

Stearne scrutinised Hopkins with a sidelong glance. Without looking around, Hopkins asked, "Something mithering you, John?"

Stearne was surprised at being caught out so effortlessly; he sat next to Hopkins and started to brush the road's dust from his boots.

"There is something mithering me, as you so ask. I noticed that you disappeared this afternoon. An urgent matter, perhaps?"

"Most urgent, Mr Stearne. Most urgent."

"As your partner, I would appreciate some candour on your part."

"Then, as my most trusted partner, you shall have it. You would appreciate that our recent visit to Stowmarket was a fruitful one. Their gratitude – financially – was an unexpected blessing for us. Such a blessing that I fear we shall soon pass from hunters to hunted."

"I don't follow."

"Think on it, Mr Stearne. With fortune comes envy. Other men's envy. The news that will be abroad in these fair counties of East Anglia will be that we were handsomely rewarded for our talents. And those handsome rewards will be filling the dreams and desires of every cutpurse, brigand and thief in this part of our glorious corner of Albion. Perhaps you now follow?"

"Someone'll rob us? But that's impossible. Our work elevates us above that, surely? People need us. They ask for us by name to help them."

Quietly chuckling, Hopkins slowly stood and blew the remaining ash from his pipe.

"I tell you most solemnly, John, that if we are set upon and robbed, we will lose more than our money. After all, we will be living witnesses to the theft and no foot soldier of the devil could ever allow that. But if we are able to show them that our monies are sparse and therefore not worth the slaying of our lives, then we have more chance of continuing with our work."

"So, what have you done with the money?"

Hopkins held a single coin up in his right hand, drew his left hand theatrically across it and then opened both empty palms to show that the coin had now vanished. Stearne, a constant witness to the conjuring of Matthew Hopkins, threw an annoyed glance back at him.

"I said, where is our money, Mr Hopkins?"

"A most pleasant spot away from both field and road. A small plantation of trees that belongs to a certain Mr Leucock."

Stearne grew increasingly agitated. "But he'll just…"

"Steal it himself? Oh, but you see, I forgot to tell the poor man that I had hidden it in his copse. Besides, I was loth to vex him, for what man could sleep at night knowing that a small fortune is secreted so close to his home. On his very own land as well. Oh no, I couldn't do that to him."

"Who else knows? What about Parsley?"

"That dunderhead? Not Parsley, not anybody. Only you, Mr Stearne, only you."

"When do we pick it up? On the way back towards Essex?"

"Ah, fair Essex. I miss home, don't you? I wonder how things fare in Mistley at this very moment. Yes, Mr Stearne, on our way back."

Both men suddenly became aware that the screaming had stopped. Stearne rebuttoned his coat whilst Hopkins flicked ash from his chest and trousers.

"So, when do we move on, Mr Hopkins? I think Kenton has given us all we're due to receive."

"All in God's own good time, Mr Stearne. There's an outstanding matter with our troublesome vicar, Mr Geffrey, that I must attend to first. Once I have satisfaction, then I will be ready to pursue our work elsewhere."

*   *   *

"Would you like more tea, Gladys?"

Gladys Cupper was staring out of the cottage window into the back garden.

"Your cabbages are coming along."

Smy glanced at the vegetable patch and smiled. "A good harvest if the caterpillars don't feast on them first."

"You think I'm mad, don't you, Fred? You think I'm making things up."

"I am not here to sit in judgment, Glad. Look, try and tell me about it again. Now that you've calmed down."

"I saw him as plain as day. As plain as you sitten there right in front of me."

"You were on the train? Where were you when you saw him? Wetheringsett? Aspall?"

"It was after Aspall. Almost at Kenton we were. He was in the wood, staring back at the train."

"How far inside the wood?"

"Not too far. A few yards, per'aps or I'd never would 'ave seen 'im. And I thought to meself, what's 'e wearen? I've not seen anyone dressed like that before. And that's when I knew."

"Knew what?"

"The Witchfinder. It was the Witchfinder. Black hat. Old black hat. Not one you'd see anyone werren nowadays. And breeches. Not trousers. They were black breeches to his knees. And then I saw 'er."

"The woman?"

A heavy sigh lurched up in the breast of Gladys Cupper and she began to quietly sob. "Oh, Fred, it was so awful. Her neck twisted. She was swaying with the wind and everything. I'm so afraid. Oh God, I'm so afraid."

Winfred Smy quickly stood and placed her comforting arms around the shoulders of Gladys Cupper who, in trying to steady herself in her seat, reached out and knocked a cup from its saucer.

"What's going to become of me, Fred? Everyone will think I'm going mad. I will be the laughing stock of Kenton. I've never felt so afraid."

Winifred Smy crouched before Gladys and held her by her arms.

"Now listen to me, Gladys. Please, just listen to me. You saw something. I believe you saw something. And no one needs to know. So let's just keep it between you and me. Understand? Here, now take this fresh hanky."

Mrs Cupper nodded, took the handkerchief and blew her nose. "Oh Fred, what would I do without you?"

Winifred Smy waited until Gladys Cupper had become calm before rising and carrying the cups and saucers to the kitchen sink. Trying not to look too interested she asked over her shoulder, "So you say it was a wood, Gladys. Which wood?"

"That small wood, when you're almost at Kenton station. It's on your right there."

"Oh, I know. Someone has just bought it. Pallant, I think his name is. I don't think he's a local man."

Through her sniffles, Mrs Cupper replied, "Yes, I think you're right."

"Well, why don't we have a walk there? Just so that I can show you that it was someone's idea of a silly joke."

"Oh, I couldn't, Fred. I couldn't go back there. Not if you paid me an 'undred sovereigns."

"Well, then, I will go. And if I do find something, I bet it explains everything. What you saw was probably just a trick of the light. Or someone trying to frighten all the passengers on the train. Did anyone else see it?"

"I don't know. I was the only one in my carriage. I don't think there were many on the train. Not many use the ol' Middy."

"Well, it only takes one other person to notice. And who knows? Perhaps you weren't the only one to see it, after all."

A knock at Winifred Smy's cottage door rudely broke into their conversation. Mrs Cupper took her cue to quickly stand up and smooth down her dress, ready to leave.

"I can't face anyone, Fred. Not looken like this. Can I leave through your back gate?"

Mrs Smy reassured her she could and, once both women had reaffirmed their vow to not tell anyone about their conversation, Gladys Cupper was soon to be seen hurrying along the road, eager to withdraw into the comforting anonymity of home.

Another series of short knocks followed and, with a shout of "Coming, coming," Winifred Smy opened the door.

Herbert Tranmer wheeled around to face her. "I had given up. I thought you were out."

He awkwardly removed his hat and held it in front of his waistcoat with both hands. Winifred Smy reddened a little, and then quickly set to restoring her usual demeanour.

"It's been a while, Inspector. Is this a social or official visit?"

"Purely social, Miss Smy. It's my day off and, as I think you know, I like to ride if the weather allows. It keeps me healthy, I hope."

"Well, that's a coincidence. I was just about to take the air myself. A brisk walk I thought. Perhaps you would care to join me?"

"Well, if you need the company."

"I don't need the company, but I would welcome your company, Inspector."

Now it was Herbert Tranmer's turn to betray a little discomfort, and Miss Smy noticed how he passed the brim of his hat through his fingers with greater speed.

"Why…" he stammered. "Where…where to, Miss Smy?"

"Oh, a lovely walk, Inspector. Why, I believe it takes in a rather charming wood."

3

Stone Cold Dead

"All saddled up, Mr Parsley? Everything in order?"

Edward Parsley was checking the tack of each horse. His usually clumsy manner always seemed strangely absent when he stood by an animal, as if a spirit of understanding entered him when he stood in their presence.

"I think so, Mr Hopkins."

"And the Albrey woman. Is she to be on her way?"

"Collected her this morning. Only got room for her at Colchester. She confessed, right enough. But was 'ard to make her do so. Mind you, we've known it take a lot longer."

"You and the searchers have bestowed on her a great act of kindness, Edward. The evils that have plagued her in this life will soon be behind her. Now we leave it to almighty God to weigh her in his celestial balance and decide whether she be found wanting."

Parsley regretfully nodded in agreement and returned to the preparations to leave.

"Mr Stearne! Do you still tarry? We must make haste now. Come, come."

Hopkins noticed that there was something rather surly in Stearne's manner, which he attributed to the conversation of the previous night. Many who encountered the pair on their travels would never have surmised that it was Stearne who was the original mover in the relationship, and Hopkins a mere assistant. But the wiliness of the latter, his effortless articulacy and brazenly self-confident manner, had all combined to elevate him to the principal role in their partnership.

"I will be with you in my own time, not yours, Mr Hopkins." There was an easily discernible tang of sarcasm in Stearne's reply.

Rumours abounded in Essex that Hopkins had once been a lawyer, but – as believable as this theory was – he never supported or denied its veracity. Whether this gradual shift in the locus of power was resented by Stearne was hard to tell, as often his silent and grudging demeanour could soon be dispelled by a sudden change to a brighter, more conciliatory manner. Such fickleness of mood served only to deepen Hopkins' distrust.

"Mr Parsley, there's daylight between the girth and the horse's belly. See to it, please!"

An indistinct, desperate shouting could be heard down the Eye Road. Everyone, as they became gradually aware of the anguished voice, turned to look down the lane; only Hopkins slowly stepped towards the source of obvious distress. As the figure – a woman running in full flight towards them with arms outstretched in front of her – drew closer, the words she was shouting slowly began to resolve themselves to an audible coherence.

"The vicar! The vicar! Mr Geffrey! He's dead. He's dead. Please, please, come and help us!"

The woman hurled herself towards Hopkins. Catching her, he gripped her by the arms.

"Be calm now. What are you talking about woman? What are you saying?"

"Mr Geffrey, Sir. He's dead. A stone fallen from the tower! Oh God!"

Hopkins, Stearne and Parsley all abandoned the caravan of animals and belongings and hurried towards the church, followed by several of the villagers. As they rushed into the churchyard they saw Henry Mouser, the churchwarden, bent over a body. Drawing closer they could see the lifeless body of Kenton's vicar, his head cruelly crushed by a large, bloodied stone that lay nearby.

"What in God's good heaven has happened here?" asked Hopkins.

Henry Mouser drew himself up to his full height and shook his head.

"I'm not sure. Logically, it seems as if one of the loose stones has fallen from the top of the tower and poor Mr Geffrey was unfortunate enough to be passing as it did so. We all knew the tower to be in great need of repair, but I never thought the stones were so loose as to visit such a calamity on someone as this."

"A most grievous calamity, indeed. Poor man. To meet such a sorry end."

"Spare me and this good man your pity, Hopkins! From what I have heard about yesterday, you and he despised each other in equal measure. I find it most strange that this tragedy should befall us whilst you blight us with your presence."

Hopkins remained curiously unmoved; his cold eyes calmly unblinking as he received the vitriol of the churchwarden, which made Mouser all the more enraged.

"Just be gone from our village! One man dead and one poor woman awaits a certain execution that you and your cronies have contrived. Your path is littered with corpses and your hands are smeared with innocent blood. A pestilence you be to all of us."

It was Stearne who responded. "You go too far, Churchwarden. This man has died through a cruel turn of fate. Our thoughts and prayers should be with him and we should rejoice that he now sits in God's great Heaven. This is not the time for emotions to curdle our words."

Rather than reply, Henry Mouser took off his jacket and laid it across the face and shoulders of the vicar. One of the villagers that had now joined the group asked, "How long 'as poor Minister been dead, Mr Mouser?"

"Long enough for his poor body to grow stiff. See how his arm sticks upward? It can only have been a few hours."

The body was moved into the church and laid before the altar; the minister's arm remained gruesomely extended out as if pointing to its heavenly destination. Hopkins and his assistants knelt, praying with a dramatic intensity before withdrawing with a sorrow that implied that the dead man had been a close and esteemed colleague. As they walked back towards the still waiting horses outside the farm, Matthew Hopkins turned to speak. "Mr Stearne, that food was much too rich last night. Why if I didn't fart twice in the church just now. My apologies if the stench offended thee."

A great guffaw of laughter went up from them all. Stearne's face remained unmoved.

*   *   *

"And how does Framlingham treat you these days, Inspector? Have you grown tired of its many pleasures, yet?"

"It suits me just fine, Miss Smy." Tranmer paused for a moment. "You seem quieter than normal. Would I be intruding if I asked why?"

"Oh, just trying to take in some rather distressing news. Something I saw in someone's paper."

"Local news, perhaps?"

Miss Smy ducked her head beneath some hawthorn branches as the path took them through a gap in a hedge. Tranmer stepped forward to hold the boughs back as she passed through.

"Most kind, Inspector."

"Herbert, please. I'm not on duty as you know."

Miss Smy looked back at him, gave one of her furiously enigmatic smiles and walked on. Tranmer caught up and asked, "You were saying about some local news you read today, Miss Smy."

"It wasn't local news at all, Inspector. It was the news that must be across every national paper in England."

"The Davison woman? The one that threw herself in front of the King's horse last week?"

"Yes, that's the news I was referring to."

"Well, it was obvious. She was not in her right mind. Whatever would make anyone throw themselves in front of a horse? What was the point she was trying to make? Just a deranged suffragette…"

"Stop right there, Inspector, or I will finish my walk alone. I knew Emily Davison. She was not deranged as you so insensitively put it. I can only think the best of her and will do so until I hear evidence to suggest otherwise."

"But all the papers…"

"Are written by the Mr Manners of this world and we all know how Mr Manners never allows facts to get in the way of his stories. No, I remain steadfast in my respect of Miss Davison and that is what troubles me."

They walked on down the footpath and watched the carriages of the Middy glide eerily along ahead of them, the rail hidden by the wheat that swayed in swerving waves before it.

"I do remember that you were part of the movement for women's votes, Miss Smy."

"You say 'were'. Is it a cause that you think I have forsaken?"

"Well, now you no longer live in London."

"Ah, so it is a London cause, you think? The fight was only for the right for women in the great metropolis to have a say in who represents them at parliament?"

"You are twisting my words and you know it."

"I am not. I am clarifying your communication. Is that not so?"

But the inspector chose not to answer; he'd become ensnared in the verbal dexterity of Winifred Smy before, and he knew when to withdraw from the intellectual joust that she seemed – almost sadistically - to enjoy. They walked on in silence, following the long curve of the hedge until it met the single railway track that hugged the contours of the field, before turning left along a wide headland.

"Is this the wood, Miss Smy?"

"It is. It now belongs to Mr Pallant. It's known locally as Low Plantation. Perhaps we might walk along its edge.

"Oh, can I just say how sorry I was to hear of your Mother's death. I had no idea. It was some months ago, I hear."

"Thank you, Mr Tranmer. It wasn't a shock, but her passing was awful to bear all the same. When both parents have died, one can feel quite alone in the world."

"I remember that she was always upstairs in the house whenever I called, but I didn't know her at all."

"Oh, even I didn't know her. Not really. No one knew her. When my father died, when I was very young, she rather withdrew into herself. She was not so much a mother as a motherly presence in many ways."

Miss Smy went ahead, slowly scrutinising the undergrowth as she did so. Some yards down the path she stopped and looked hard into the wood. Much of the ferns and grasses that formed the forest undergrowth lay broken, as if someone had been trampling heavily over them. Slowly, holding her skirt slightly aloft with her hands, she entered the wood and started to peer penetratingly around her. She took two steps to her right and, bending down, pushed away some broken shrubs before reaching towards the ground.

"Found something, Miss Smy?" asked a bemused Herbert Tranmer.

Miss Smy turned towards the Inspector and held up a rope.

4

No Stone Unturned

"A stoat, you say?"

"Yes, indeed, Mr Pilbeam. Running right across your lawn. Quite caught me off my guard." replied Winifred Smy.

The vicar pulled up a chair to the desk and invited her to sit down. She did so whilst glancing at the many books that lined the far wall of his study.

"Ah, I forgot that you remain a voracious reader, Miss Smy. If you see something that tickles your reading fancy then please feel free to take it with you. I was rather taken with *Swann's Way* by a French author I've not come across before. I can't decide whether it was tedious or over-thoughtful. Probably both."

"Who is the author?"

"Prest? Prust? Oh, let me see…" Pilbeam walked briskly to the bookshelf and, raising his glasses from his eyes to his forehead, looked at the book's spine. "Proust! That's the fellow. Here, take it and let me know what you think." He handed her the book and returned to his desk seat, opposite Miss Smy.

"I shall enjoy having a go," said Miss Smy. "Now, you said you wanted to see me? Are you already thinking about the Harvest Festival? We're barely a month into Pentecost."

"Oh no, Miss Smy. Much too early for that. Some days ago, I had a visitor. An anxious visitor who claims to have seen a ghost. From the train apparently. Just coming into Kenton."

Miss Smy nodded very slowly as she took in the news. "Was it Mrs Cupper? I am reluctant to ask you this as she had asked for my complete discretion."

The Reverend Pilbeam leaned back in his chair and smiled mischievously, "The very same. She told me that you were the only other person who knew, and I asked her if I might discuss the matter with you. She assented, of course."

"Yes, she shared the apparition with me also. She was convinced she had seen a witchfinder and a woman hanging from a tree. I had promised not to tell anyone, but she seems to have confided in you also. Do you believe there is anything for us to discuss?"

The vicar sprang from his chair and looked out of the window behind his desk. "Well, yes and no, Miss Smy."

"Are you trying to be enigmatic, Mister Pilbeam?"

A great roar of laughter erupted from Pilbeam, who returned to his seat. "I fear I'm too rational to ever be called 'enigmatic'; but I would also say the same for you. We are two rather practical souls."

"*Touché*, Sir. Perhaps you would share your 'yes' and your 'no'?"

The reverend looked studiedly at Miss Smy for some moments, considering how best to start.

"The ghost? Oh, that's definitely my 'no'. Probably just a trick of the light. We've all had it. You see a crow on a branch but find, as you get close to it, that it's a large field-hand's glove that's been forgotten. Easily done. Perhaps Mrs Cupper has been under some strain lately?"

"Not to my knowledge. Of all the people in Kenton, I would say she has the most robust constitution, mentally and physically."

Pilbeam sat up. "So you believe her?"

"I don't say I believe what she saw, but I am reluctant to say that she saw nothing."

"Now it's your turn to be enigmatic. Help me out here: you don't think she saw a ghost, but you are saying that she saw something?"

"What I am saying is that I think she might have seen something but, like you, I do not believe in ghosts."

"Hmm. Then you bring me to my 'yes'."

Winifred Smy's face suddenly became serious. "You intrigue me."

Pilbeam rose once more from his chair and opened the lid of a mahogany writing desk that stood in the corner of his study. He carefully selected a document and returned to his seat. "As you know, the church is rather fond of bureaucracy so papers and whatnot regularly appear from many a nook and cranny. Most are old bills and so forth, but occasionally a real gem turns up." As he said this, he held up a carefully folded sheet of paper, now quite yellowed with age.

"And this gem of a document is your 'yes'?" asked Miss Smy.

"It is indeed. Some years before I became the incumbent of this illustrious parish, our church of All Saints was rather heavily restored. Most of the restoration was sensitive enough, although the chancel window was – if I may say so – architecturally unwise. Hakewill, I think the man's name was. Good fellow by all accounts and I have deigned to forgive him the dreadful chancel window. But – and here's the interesting bit – secreted in the corner of the chantry chapel, he found a letter."

"To whom?"

"To the future."

"I'm not sure what you're driving at. Are you saying it was written for someone to read after this person had died?"

"Quite so. A sort of message in a bottle, like those desert island chaps write, when waiting to be rescued. When I first read it, I could see it was written by someone claiming to be the old churchwarden of our church. Henry Mouser was the fellow's name, but I wasn't sure if it wasn't some sort of hoax. Perhaps this Hakewill had a strange sense of humour. So I rifled through the records of the previous churchwardens and there he was: Henry Mouser. Fascinating, eh?"

"Indeed."

"Next, I took it to an old University chum who now lives in Essex. He asked me to leave it with him for a week or so. History is his thing, and he was all over the letter like a shot. Told me that he'd spent the best part of a day looking up names and the like and gave Mouser's account a right royal thumbs up. Even told me that the writing was done with a goose quill on paper made from cotton or linen rags or some such. If it was a hoax, it would be a rather extraordinary one."

"Who else have you shared the letter with?"

"Not a soul. To be honest, I'd rather put it all out of my mind, until Miss Cupper's strange testimony made me return to it. And I must admit to now finding it rather curious."

Pilbeam, fired by the dramatic narrative he was revealing, looked at Miss Smy to register what effect he'd achieved so far. He pushed the letter towards her but kept his hands lightly upon it.

"And this is the letter?"

"It is. Would you like to read it?"

Miss Smy pulled her chair closer to the desk. Pilbeam lifted his hands away.

*   *   *

"With trust in Jesus Christ for the forgiveness of sins, and through his most precious blood, I write the following account so that an earthly justice may be obtained through it.

My name is Henry Mouser and, until very recently, I had the great privilege of being churchwarden to All Saints Church, Kenton. Being now in my 73rd year and with failing strength yet remaining sound and disposing of mind, I know that my God will call me home very soon. Yea, I know it and welcome it heartily.

I have lived through much: plague, civil war, regicide, and a king's restoration. Yet I am daily troubled by one singular instance that happened in my beloved village in the year 1647. Whilst this country fought a bloody and foul war, with English brother slaying English brother, a pestilence of thought descended upon this land and wickedness and evil beset us. One manifestation of that evil was a man who is now long dead, Matthew Hopkins.

In the summer of the year I have mentioned, 1647, a group of villagers of this parish had heard it told of a Witchfinder who could prove with certainty whether a mortal woman was in league with Satan. You may think as I did and still do, that such work is mere charlatanry and preys upon the weak and infirm. I would not countenance such abhorrent views and made this known to all who might listen. But my voice was a lone one and, try as I might, others in Kenton were swayed by the empty sophistry of others.

One dark day that summer, Elizabeth Albrey was dragged from her house by Matthew Hopkins, John Stearne and their henchmen and subjected to examinations of her person to establish whether she was a witch or not. What took place in that farmhouse, where she was stripped and demeaned, I will never know – and I thank God for it. Their labours were rewarded when they claimed that, even when the searchers pricked her with a bodkin needle, she felt no pain. This, they confirmed, was evidence and they made haste to repair her to Colchester where she was to be detained before they hanged her. God rest that poor woman's soul.

I knew Elizabeth Albrey, in youth and in age, and she was no witch. Like many who, with God's grace, survive to an old age, her wits had departed her, and she became much unstable in mind. But a witch? No, by all that's sacred and holy, she was never a witch. But this is not the incident that vexes me still. Elizabeth Albrey, I am certain, now resides in the celestial home of our redeemer; her agony long ceased.

Yet now I must turn to another dark deed that lies beyond my understanding, and one which I have perpetually turned over in my mind.

I mentioned the humiliating spectacle of one of our Kenton brethren being evicted – like the lowliest criminal - from her own home and placed before the sneering sinners who had brought Hopkins and Stearne to our village. I was not there as I was in attendance to an ailing parishioner on a distant farm. I have heard from several witnesses that our own vicar, the able and good man that was Minister Geffrey who, upon hearing of the disgraceful scenes I have already related, made great haste to Elizabeth Albrey's house and pleaded for her safety. Hopkins heeded him not and taunted him with recent events at Brandeston, where another minister of our faith was accused of a similar satanic discourse with the devil and most sorrowfully was hanged for it.

That afternoon, I met the minister in the nave of our church. I knew him to be a man of unimpeachable integrity and feeling. I watched for a little time as he quietly prayed in his humble way. Afterwards, we fell to talking and he told me the hideous events that had occurred that morning within the very boundaries of our parish. He looked a broken man, for he had witnessed for himself how rational thought can be humbled by a Godless, vacuous, and cruel sentiment. I think what smote him deepest was to watch these atrocities take place with the supposed blessing of our beneficent and ever-loving God.

We parted in the graveyard and repaired to our respective homes. I was not to see that dear man alive again.

The very next morning, I made my way, as usual, to our church as we have a chest for alms and, as one of the three keepers of the keys to unlock it, I was due to meet Minister Geffrey and John Clodd for its inspection. As I turned in from Church Lane towards the church, I beheld a pitiful sight. At the foot of the tower lay the body of Minister Geffrey. His head most severely bloodied and a large stone close by. I could see that he was dead for no man could survive such a terrible wound. For a reason I know not, Minster Geffrey's arm was outstretched in a ghastly manner.

Master Clodd and I were soon joined by Margaret Cotwin. She took great fright at the cruel demise of Minister Geffrey and fled the scene in agitated and great distress. Some few minutes later, Hopkins and his retinue appeared, affecting to be much shocked by what they saw. We opened the church and moved the body into the chancel and – with as much respect as we could muster – laid him thereto.

I am not a foolish man, I have already related that I have seen too much in my life, and I was not fooled by the great pretence of display by Hopkins and his lackeys. It was the form of basest mummery that they did show and, in their arrogance, were minded that others would not see it. I despised every moment in their company. Those that served the witchfinders were not to be trusted, especially one known as Edward Parsley. There was something about him that brought Luke's words to mind, "He that is unjust in the least is unjust also in much."

When all had gone, Mr Clodd and I returned to the base of the tower, and it was here that I was struck by a most singular feature. Upon the stone there was a small deal of blood, but it did not seem consistent with the deep gouging blow that had felled Minister Geffrey. I drew the attention of Master Clodd to the stone and sought his counsel. I put it to him that it must have fallen from the tower as the stones at the top had worked loose over the years. But he expressed astonishment that this would be so. He knew the tower's stonework well, and this stone was not part of the fabric of the walls.

It was then that another thought came upon me. Minister Geffrey was lying close to the tower wall. But why? There was no necessity to walk beside it and, if he had been inspecting it, the coincidence that a heavy stone should fall upon him at that very moment is difficult for any rational man to accept.

All this troubled me deeply and I shared my doubts with Master Clodd. He confessed to being similarly astonished but could find no other reason than the fact that Minister Geffrey had been struck dead by the stone when it had worked loose from the tower and fell.

Now that my suspicions had been so resolutely raised, I found myself returning to the contorted stiffness of the arm of the dead man. In battle, when I served in the 13th troop of Ralph Margery, a good and brave man from Walsham le Willows, I saw many a man bludgeoned by a heavy blow, and when they fell, they crumpled flat along the ground. Not once have I witnessed a body whose limb extended as did Minister Geffrey.

Master Clodd and I took the stone and placed it at the buttress by the south porch. It lies there still for none will remove it out of respect for our much-loved vicar. Every day I pass it and seek answers to these doubts. If it wasn't an accident, then it must be the one heinous crime that offends a sacred commandment: thou shalt not kill. To this day I remain strongly minded that Minister Geffrey was not slain by a cruel coincidence, but by the hand of a wicked mortal. But how am I to prove this? It is not within my power to seek the true justice this person deserves. I must trust in my God that his will shall be done.

I have waylaid you enough, reader, with these memories. I am prepared for the everlasting glory of the kingdom of Heaven and hope that it will take this hunger for truth from me. I am done with unloading my much-vexed mind and leave this note to a wiser posterity.

Pray for my soul; I will soon recommend it to God that gave it.

Henry Mouser

In the year of our Lord, 1671."

*   *   *

Miss Smy gently placed the letter down. Pilbeam had been reading her face as she took in each sentence.

"Well, Miss Smy. What do you think?"

"I think I would welcome a strong cup of tea."

"Oh, I'll get Hannah to see to that. But do you know what the strange thing is? The one fact that almost makes our hands reach across time and touch the very hands of Henry Mouser?"

"Do tell."

"That stone. The stone that felled our gallant Mr Geffrey is still there. In exactly the same place that Mouser and Clodd left it."

5

Let Sleeping Stones Lie

The leaves that fringed the churchyard oaks had lost the lime freshness that spring had first bestowed and were now hardening into a deeper green that would see them through the summer. Around the graves, meadow buttercups genuflected airily on their long stems, and spikes of blue-purple self-heal insinuated themselves amongst the long grass. Winifred Smy and Reverend Pilbeam walked thoughtfully along the path to the south porch of All Saints Church, the latter gently teasing Miss Smy.

"Surely that's what Parliament is for, Miss Smy? To decide these matters on our behalf."

"How can the two chambers of Parliament, consisting almost entirely of entitled, desiccated male fossils understand the needs or rights of women? Make no mistake, the laws they seek to enact are those that place heavier shackles on our liberties. After all, what sort of democracy..."

But Miss Smy's reproval was cut short as she caught sight of the stone: a large round boulder, its colour somewhere between a light brown and a dull pink. It sat at the foot of the porch's buttress like a large football discarded by some long-departed ogre.

"This is the stone?"

"Indeed," replied the vicar.

"How do you know it's the same stone? I've never noticed it before and I've been walking through this churchyard most of my life. It could have been rolled there at any time."

Pilbeam crouched down to inspect it. "Old man Nesling calls it 'The Priest Killer'. Apparently, his grandfather always told him old yarns about it crushing the skull of some unfortunate vicar back in Cromwell's day. Locals were adamant that if you moved it, you would die within the week. That seems to have somewhat discouraged the churchwardens to move it elsewhere."

"I find such stories rather tenuous, I'm afraid. As full of air as village gossip."

Still crouched over the stone and looking closely at its surface, Pilbeam replied, "Perhaps I am not quite as practical as I said earlier. I have often found that such stories are rooted in something much deeper. Of course, each storyteller unfailingly burnishes the silver of the tale with each retelling, but a deeper truth lies within all the same."

Pilbeam now stood up, removed his hat, and scratched the crown of his wiry hair. "When Hakewill - you remember, the architect fellow I was talking about - was inflicting his monstrosity on the east wall of our chancel, a fellow called Schliemann was busying himself with the silly notion that the legendary city of Troy was actually real. Of course, everyone thought he was just some madman wandering the Turkish landscape with a spade and a heavily annotated copy of Homer. But, dash it all, the blighter was right! He found his Troy. And if Turkey can have its Troy, then surely Kenton can have its stone?"

"Can you lift it up?"

"I've never tried. Besides, are you asking me to test the validity of the prophecy? If I do, I might not see the month out and we handsome vicars are in short supply."

Winifred Smy stooped down and, with an energy that was one part muscle and one part impatience, jerked the stone backwards to reveal a still-moist bed of earth beneath. Agitated woodlice and a coppery centipede were galvanised with panic, instantly seeking the sanctuary of the stone's encircling grass.

"Ah, *Lithobius forficatus,* Miss Smy. Despite its rather unprepossessing form, a friend to all gardeners nonetheless."

Miss Smy stood up and wiped her hands. She stared hard at the stone as if doing so would reveal its secrets. "Where did Henry Mouser say Mr Geffrey was found?"

"I'm afraid he was disappointingly vague on that matter. 'At the foot of the tower' was, if my grey matter serves me correctly, the only information he communicated."

Winifred Smy stepped backwards, looked up and took in the full height of the tower. Despite having lived so close to the church for most of her life, she now studied it anew. A high horizontal band of stone circles sat just below the crenellated parapet. Following the line of her gaze, Pilbeam placed his hat back upon his head and asked, "A penny for your musings, Miss Smy?"

"I take it the church would have been locked before Mr Geffrey arrived?"

"One would assume so. But who knows? The world might have been a kinder place in his day. It might have remained open for private prayer. However, the question we must answer is: did this stone kill Minister Geffrey?"

Miss Smy looked once more at the stone. "No, I don't think so."

"Enlighten me, Miss Smy. Why ever not?"

"I find it impossible to accept that the stone was dislodged – either by fate or human hand – and fell upon our Mr Geffrey. Even the oldest parts of this tower are flint rubble, and such a large stone would never have been incorporated into its fabric."

Pilbeam nodded his assent. "So, we discount Mr Geffrey's tragic demise by our Priest Killer here. And I agree, a stone this size and of this material would never have been an original part of the stonework."

Miss Smy placed her hand against the tower and proceeded to slowly walk along its girth. She felt the warmth of the flint beneath her palm and dragged her open hand along its scratched and sculptured surfaces.

"What about this door?" Miss Smy inspected the entrance that allowed access to the tower.

Pilbeam had removed his hat once more and was diverted by the sounds of the gentle June winds nonchalantly blowing against his face. "Hmm? What door?"

"The West door here. Was this door locked?"

"My dear Miss Smy, how in heaven would I know? I wasn't there on the fateful day. Have pity for God's sake. These events occurred over two hundred and fifty years ago. Even my empathy for Kenton's historical heritage has its limits."

Smy smiled and continued to walk around the tower until she was on the north side of the church. Her attention immediately turned to a modest headstone at the very edge of the graveyard. She brought both of her hands up on either side of her face and looked at the grave with an acute intensity. The Reverend Pilbeam, now catching up with her, immediately perceived where her mind had travelled. With a sensitivity that belied his usually dismissive air, he turned his steps back to the path and pretended to find a deep fascination in the commonplace flora of the churchyard.

Winifred Smy felt the harsh weight of grief gather once more in her chest and yet, nonetheless, still walked towards the headstone; the brash brightness of the stone had yet to be dulled by the relentless years of weathering that would eventually assail it.

The banked earth that lay before her mother's grave had almost become level with the surrounding terrain. She sat beside what remained of the mound, leaned against the stone that bore the simple facts of her mother's recent extinction and looked upwards at the sky. Swifts turned and tumbled; wispy shreds of clouds drifted with an insolent slowness. Miss Smy grabbed at a sedge, tightening her grip around it before violently pulling it clear of the earth and then letting it fall. In that moment, all was perfectly silent and still.

Some few minutes later, at the far end of the churchyard, a pony and trap could be heard but not seen. An aggrieved voice was admonishing the driver's rates and an irritable exchange then followed. Threats – expressed in low and indistinct voices

– ensued before an ominous silence emerged. The pony and trap slowly moved off.

Through the gap that marked the eastern entrance into the churchyard, appeared Nigel Manners, a local journalist that Miss Smy secretly loathed yet grudgingly admired in equal measure. He stopped and placed his hands in his waistcoat like a preening headmaster addressing a hall of precocious pupils. Seeing Winifred Smy, he raised his hand and immediately walked towards her, but found the realisation that she was recumbent by her mother's grave rather alarming. By imperceptible degrees his long, awkward strides slowed to the gentlest of steps as he approached.

Miss Smy watched him as he came nearer and said, "Do you know, Mr Manners, I think it was Walter Scott who once wrote, 'The hour's come, and the man.'"

*   *   *

"You there! Which way to Diss?" But the woman, frightened at the strange group of men and women, warily drew back before running into her small cottage, closing and bolting the door behind her. This was immediately followed by her stuffing rags into the small apertures that served as the only windows of her mean home.

"Where are we, Parsley?" asked Hopkins.

"Stuston, I'd say."

"Stuston, eh? And how far to Diss?"

"I reckon two or three mile. The road we've followed is the right way. These cart ruts tell me it's probably a well-used cut-through from the Roman Road back there."

Hopkins looked around at the sparse arrangement of rude dwellings, their uneven walls springing from the rampant clumps of weeds that clustered to them. Further ahead, a dog walked wearily across the lane as if drained of all energy by the steadily rising heat of the June sun. Innumerable flies danced, settled, scratched and bit the visitors, causing horses to shake their heads and riders to slap their necks and cheeks to be rid of them.

Matthew Hopkins was just about to gather the reins of his horse to continue the journey when he saw Frances Mills walking awkwardly towards him.

"Sir?"

"Yes, Frances. What is it?" he testily replied.

"When we get to Diss, could I speak with you? There's something that's been weighin' on my mind."

"Does it have to wait, woman? Can you not just tell me now?"

Frances Mills shifted uneasily on her feet and kept her eyes to the floor. She remained painfully conscious of the cowpox scars that were an unsightly legacy of her previous employment as a milkmaid. "I wanted to keep it atween us, if you don't mind, Sir."

"We will have no secrets amongst us, Frances. Whatever it is, openly share it to all."

Frances Mills threw the slightest of glances to the others behind and began to rub her neck in an acute embarrassment. "Well, it was that Elizabeth Albrey. Of course, I didn't acquaint along o' she, but she screamed something that I can't get out of my head."

Hopkins, seeing how troubled his searcher was, dismounted and removed his gloves before placing a hand gently on her shoulder. "The word of almighty God tells us that, 'Lying lips are abomination to the Lord: but they that deal truly are his delight'. If what you want to speak is the truth, then deal truly with me."

"Well, of course she were dawzled by what we had done with her, and haps she was sorft in the hid, but she do suddenly woke up and cried out. She shouted, 'A curse on Matthew Hopkins! A curse on 'im! One day he'll drown and die in his own blood, I do swear it!'"

Hopkins remained silent for some moments, but it was plain to everyone there that something had penetrated his usually impervious, haughty demeanour.

"Rantings, dear Frances. That's all. Just the rantings of a devil woman. Such things do not vex me. You know your proverbs, I'm sure: 'The lip of truth shall be established for ever: but a lying tongue is but for a moment'. Now, my good woman, let's resume our sojourn with haste."

Frances gave a slight bow of her head and withdrew whilst Hopkins remounted his horse. As they trudged away from the village, Hopkins' face was troubled. What his companions weren't to know was that, some weeks ago, as he'd finished washing his face, a sudden need to cough had seized him and he had gathered and spat out the phlegm that had collected in his throat.

There, unmistakably there, was a streak of ruby blood encased within the sputum. He knew the colour of that blood and what it foretold.

6

God or Mammon?

"A most toothsome cake and no mistake!" Nigel Manners proceeded to methodically suck the tip of each finger, determined that no single crumb might escape.

"Then I will wrap what remains and put it aside for your journey back to Framlingham," replied a satisfied Winifred Smy.

Manners showed his evident delight in her offer by awkward jerks of both elbows, pulling them into his body as if they were ill-fitting wings; as he did this, his shoulders smoothly rose and fell, quite independent of each other.

"You are too kind, Miss Smy. But I fear your cake has a price tag on it?"

Winifred Smy sat down and sipped her tea, her eyes watching Manners over the brim of her cup.

"Mr Manners, despite my initial impression of you, I believe you are a man of exceptional talents."

"Miss Smy, first your delicious cake, then your compliments. I feel you are preparing me for some Herculean task. I hope I'm not being presumptuous at this point. But you must understand that my obsessive purpose is news and, unless you can prove that the task contains something of interest for our beloved readers, then I must respectfully step away from what you desire me to do, excellent cake notwithstanding."

"Come, come, Mr Manners. Your remarks are not worthy of one who calls himself a journalist. I know nothing of the newspaper world; that you will agree with I am sure. But I do know that having access to an exciting story whilst it is still unfolding - and being the first to report it - does wonders for one's standing and prospects."

Nigel Manners said nothing, but his head jerked like an inquisitive blackbird watching a gardener turning over fresh soil. His lips repeatedly pursed forward and then pulled back again, but the eyes – as they ever did – never left those of Miss Smy.

Miss Smy placed her cup on its saucer before moving both items of crockery to one side. "I have a friend, Mr Manners, a most reliable person of sound common sense. They were recently returning on The Middy to Kenton when, some quarter of a mile or so before our station, they saw a man standing in a wood."

"But it was no ordinary man, I propose, or else you would not be mentioning it."

"Your perspicacity does you credit, Mr Manners. The man in question was dressed as a witchfinder: stovepipe hat, riding boots, in fact wearing all the accoutrements of a man from the 17th century."

Manners closed one eye and trained the other at Miss Smy in a rather disconcerting manner. It was almost as if this was the organ through which the information was being received rather than his ears. Although slightly unnerved by this new tic of her interlocutor, she decided to continue.

"When I first was told about this I, despite my long years of knowing this person and having the utmost regard for their integrity, dismissed it as probably some visual misapprehension. But they were adamant and I found it hard to dissuade them otherwise."

"They were quite sure?"

"Oh, yes, quite sure."

"A prankster? A farmer with a penchant for dressing up in historical garb, perhaps? Surely these are adequate suppositions that would easily explain away what your friend saw?"

"But that wasn't all they saw that day. A very short distance from the man – this witchfinder - was a woman hanging from a tree."

Manners' lips were now so pushed forward that the upper of the pair met with the tip of his long nose.

"Hanging, you say? By the neck?"

"Is there any other way that someone might be hanged?"

Manners pursed his lips once more but now closed his seeing eye and reopened the other.

"Who knows about this, Miss Smy? Obviously, you and your friend, of course. But anyone else?"

"Only our vicar, Mr Pilbeam."

"The man in the churchyard with you, when I first saw you?"

Winifred Smy nodded. Nigel Manners sprang like a flea from his chair and walked along the back wall of the small kitchen, to and fro, occasionally glancing at Miss Smy.

"Curious," he muttered. "So very curious. But dash it all, it might still be a prank? And this…friend of yours, despite your high opinion, might have been sleeping on the train and in their confused waking state as the train approached the station, dreamt that they saw this…this horrific vision."

"Quite possibly. Except for the fact that I took the trouble of going to the spot where my friend saw those two figures. Sure enough, it was quite apparent that the vegetation had been recently disturbed and…" Winifred Smy broke off her sentence and went into her hall, re-emerging with the rope that she had found. "…I discovered this."

Manners took the rope and inspected it as closely as an antiquarian runs an experienced eye over a fine porcelain Ming vase.

"This wood. The place where your friend thinks they saw all of this. Has it a name?"

"Low Plantation. It belongs to a Mr Pallant. Apparently, he now owns a little land around here."

"Is he local?"

"I don't think so. An Ipswich man, I think. In fact, it was only two or three months ago that anybody had ever heard of him."

"Anyone met him, Miss Smy?"

"He's rather a mystery to us all, although I do have one person in my acquaintance who might shed a little light."

Nigel Manners handed the rope back to Miss Smy, his long arms telescopically sliding out from his sleeves as he did so.

"You've not told anyone else about this. You're quite sure?"

"Quite sure," Miss Smy called from the hall where she was now returning the rope to its safe place of keeping.

"But your friend. Perhaps they might have told someone else? Have you thought about that?"

"I have, Mr Manners. I am not going to reassure you any more about who is, and who is not, party to what I have told you."

"Not even Inspector Tranmer?"

Miss Smy was caught short by this question and hesitated. "No, no I am certain he doesn't know. He accompanied me to the wood where I found the rope but knows nothing else for the moment."

"For the moment?"

"I might discreetly share what I know at a time of my own choosing to certain people who may assist my endeavours, Mr Manners. I think that that is an approach you might respect?"

"Of course. Quite so. Well, this afternoon has proved to be both delightful and intriguing."

Winifred Smy led Mr Manners through the front door and out into the small garden.

"I'm not a spiritual person, Mr Manners. I have no religious convictions and am minded to believing only what can be empirically substantiated. But there is something in this that disturbs me. I don't know what or why. I can offer no explanation. But a missive brought to my attention by Reverend Pilbeam only today has served to augment my sense of disquiet."

"My answer is yes."

Miss Smy, who had become lost in her thoughts, looked up and said, "Sorry? Yes to what?"

"To your request for my services, Miss Smy! As you said in the churchyard, 'The hour's come, and the man.' Have faith, good lady, for I am your man!"

Manners turned sharply and, with his thin limbs coordinating themselves as best they could, he walked down the road towards Framlingham. Within minutes, he had hailed a farmer's horse and cart that were moving in the same direction and, with the promise of a few pennies for his fare, jumped on to the back of the cart from which he waved to Miss Smy.

When Winifred Smy walked back into her house a curious thought struck her. Why had Mr Manners come to Kenton today? He had never once explained the reason for his visit. Was it serendipity that had brought him to the churchyard that afternoon? Or was it that Mr Manners knew much more than he was letting on?

*   *   *

"Mr Stearne, I respectfully suggest that we should return to journeying separately. It has been most rewarding to spend time with you again, but the devil's forces have been unleashed in too many villages and we are but one regiment when we ride together. At least let us revert to separate units to double our resistance to Satan."

John Stearne, having enjoyed his meal and now sitting back in his chair, eyed Hopkins warily. "I appear to have finished my drink. Innkeeper! Innkeeper!"

It wasn't the Innkeeper who appeared but his daughter, a small, plump girl of thirteen or fourteen years whose immediate presence had a pleasing effect on Stearne. He smiled obsequiously and tried to grab her as she moved around his chair to take his pewter mug, but she had - even in one so young – long experience in avoiding the lascivious grasps of customers in various states of drunkenness.

"A pretty one, so you are. God produces some fine work, and there is none finer than you, I swear."

Matthew Hopkins brought his own empty mug fiercely down onto the table, bringing Stearne's alarmed attention back to him whilst allowing the girl the means of escape. "Mr Stearne, please turn your mind to my question! Your conduct is most unseemly. We are foot soldiers of God, and your behaviour must befit our calling."

Stearne fell back into silence for some moments, before peevishly saying, "And where will your journey be extending to? Perhaps you have reason to return to Kenton? You seemed to find it a delightful place. So much so, that you admitted to wandering its elysian meadows and woods. I thought it dismal, but you are a man of refined tastes and see so much more than I."

Hopkins glowered at Stearne. "I will push North. Maybe to the coast. Only yesterday you enthused that the west of Suffolk promises work that will suit your talents. Do not trifle with me, Mr Stearne. Your oblique and, if I may say, entirely unwarranted references to the money I have hidden is most unbecoming from a man of your stature."

Stearne pushed himself away from the table, barely able to contain his deep annoyance.

"But it is our money, Mr Hopkins! Our money! And you took it upon yourself to hide it in a place only you know of. Tell me, sir, tell me this: what if something was to happen to you? Where would we all be then? Our work is fraught with danger, and we travel through counties that teem with the wicked and ungodly. That money is our reward on earth and you, you…"

"Lower your voice, Mr Stearne. It is incumbent on us that we carry ourselves with the requisite degree of decorum amongst these baser people."

Stearne resentfully walked to the window, smeared and dirty with the patina of years of greasy candle smoke, and stared at the yard outside.

Hopkins, his anger slowly subsiding, rose from his own chair and walked over to Stearne.

"John, John. You do me a great disservice. My intention was always to tell you where the money is. You are right, my friend. It is indeed our reward. The fault lies with me. But my intention was honourable. If we were indeed set upon by some band of rapscallions, it would have been me that was tortured into revealing its place. I wouldn't wish that upon any of you and, stupidly I now admit, I believed that it would have saved your lives not to know."

Stearne moved away and returned to his chair.

"My dear Mr Hopkins, what troubles me is that, over time, people have increasingly seen you as somehow the general of our army. When we first began our struggles in Manningtree, we sat side by side. There was no fear nor favour, not one above the other. But, as time has marched on, I have not failed to notice a shifting in our positions and, for I must be truthful about this, you have acted in a way that only confirms my suspicions."

"But I have told you where I secreted our money. A plantation belonging to some Mr Leucock. Surely you remember that?"

"How big is this plantation? If, God forbid, something was to happen to you, I would be required to turn over every inch of it until I found the coins. I don't even know where this plantation is!"

"Then I shall tell you everything. You'll remember the church back in Kenton? There is a small lane to one side of it that leads to Debenham. No more than half a mile from the church is the place I have hidden our money. Here, let me show you." Hopkins stooped down and started to draw a map in the sawdust.

"Here is the lane from the church. The road will turn a sharp left and very quickly, a sharp right. Go past the entrance to a farm on your right and you will soon come to where the lane turns another sharp left. At this turn is a smaller lane to your right which you must take."

"Is this lane wide enough to ride along?"

"Oh, easily. The lane comes out in a field at which you must turn left and follow a field path. It is easy enough to track and carries on into a second field. Ahead of you will be Mr Leucock's plantation. There is a small rectangle of trees to your right, but, as you enter the wood, you must locate yourself at a mid-point along the edge of the larger section of wood on your left. From there, you will see that you can walk fifteen paces into the wood without hindrance from any of the trees."

"What should I be looking for?"

"Within that wood is a mature beech. You will know it by a cross that I have etched on to its trunk on the opposite side. It is on that side of the beech that you will find the money buried, a few inches down or so, no more than that."

John Stearne stared at the map and memorised what Hopkins had drawn in the sawdust. He then drew his hand across it so that all trace of the route disappeared. "Thank you for your candour, Matthew. I think your suggestion that we part and go our separate ways at this point is a sound one."

A knock at the door told both men that it must be one of their own, for the landlord and his staff had no reservation about moving freely about their hostelry.

"Come!" ordered Hopkins.

Edward Parsley pushed open the door and, with head bowed, entered the room.

"Beggin' your pardons, Sir, but the horses are abed."

"And the searchers? Where are they?"

"Good lodgings, Sir. They will sleep well."

"Thank you, Mr Parsley. You may retire as well."

Whilst Parsley withdrew, John Stearne rose from his chair and remained still at the head of the table.

"My demeanour has been rather unseemly of late, I admit. But these are troubling times and I fear that I am somewhat unsettled in my spirits. I seek your forgiveness if my behaviour falls short of my ambition."

"I accept your apology, Mr Stearne, but I would ask you to carry Matthew's verse in your heart: 'No man can serve two masters: for either he will hate the one, and love the other; or else he will hold to the one, and despise the other. Ye cannot serve God and mammon.'"

"An eloquent biblical argument, Mr Hopkins. But it is mammon that pays my bills."

7

A Dawzled Spadger

The violent commotion that Miss Smy could hear from within The Dove public house told her all she needed to know. Sure enough, the front door was pulled back and a small man was hurtled out onto the unforgiving pavement.

"That'll larn yer!" shouted a peremptory voice from inside the pub's porch.

Miss Smy picked up the ejected party's crumpled hat and brushed some of the dust from it. Having rolled over on the hard surface several times, the man now slowly sat up and came to terms with his new, less convivial surroundings. It was at this point that he noticed Winifred Smy; he went to raise his hat in acknowledgement, only to find that very item of headwear was missing.

"Is this what you're looking for, Spadger?"

"Miss Smy! How yew a' diddl'n?"

"I'm very well. Mrs Corner seems to have had enough of your provocative conversation for one day?"

"Oh, I wuz just leaven anyway. Soon be time for beavers."

"Are you hurt?"

"Well, I hooly jinked my leg when I fell over. Bit dawzled per'aps."

Miss Smy helped Spadger Peck get to his feet and he carefully returned his hat to his grizzled grey head at an angle that seemed to convey all his mischievousness and guile.

"I'm glad I caught you, Spadger. Are you walking home? It would be good to walk some of the way with you."

Spadger Peck checked his tatty clothing with the keen eye of a Jermyn Street gentleman's tailor. After a final minor correction of his jacket sleeve, he harrumphed an approval to show that his exacting sartorial standards were now satisfied. With the most respectful of bows he indicated with an outstretched arm that Miss Smy should proceed up Debenham's High Street.

"I have a question about something and could think of no better person who might answer it than you. It's to do with Low Plantation."

"Out Kenton way?"

"The very same. I understand that a Mr Pallant purchased it some months back?"

"S'right. Good'rh'm sold it to 'im. Thas a rum 'un why Pallant bought it. Paid too much, if yew ask me."

"Ah, it was Mr Gooderham's wood? Why did he want to sell it?"

"Don't think 'e did. My understanden is Mr Pallant asked 'im to name a proice. Paid a fortune for 'em all. Not just Low Plantation, but Leucock and Bellwell Plantation an' all."

"Oh, so he bought the two other plantations as well? He must have wanted to buy them very badly."

Spadger Peck stood still for a moment and then looked up at Miss Smy, his eyes creased with thought.

"Something wrong, Spadger?"

"Miss Smy, you know I drink a good tidy lot of jumble, so my memory is not what it wuz. But there wuz suffen strange about Mr Pallant."

"You've met him?"

Spadger nodded. "Cherry Tree. At's a proper pub that is. Not like what she runs at The Dove. Why that Mrs Corner…she's tew maggoty to run a proper pub."

Winifred Smy could sense that the considerable intake of alcohol Spadger had enjoyed was blurring his line of thought.

"So, what happened? When you met Mr Pallant?"

"Hmm? Oh, he bought me a drink. Asked a lot of questions. Questions about the woods off Bellwell Lane. But 'e knew ort about farmen. He imitate to be a farmer, but he wuz no farmer. Must 'ave thought I wuz sorft in the hid."

"Why do you think he was so interested in the woods off Bellwell Lane?"

Miss Smy motioned to Spadger to walk on, very aware that certain villagers were intrigued – though not surprised – by her choice of afternoon company.

"Search me, Miss Smy. Nothing special about any of 'em. Might use 'em for pightles, per'aps."

"Tell me, if he wasn't a farmer, then what was he? His job, I mean?"

Spadger Peck rubbed his chin hard as he thought. "Now what 'e say 'e was? Told me roight enow. Moosician! Thas it!"

"A musician? Are you sure?"

"Moosician," repeated Spadger Peck. "Still doin' it, 'e said."

For some unknown reason, Miss Smy wasn't expecting such an answer. She didn't know why, but there was some vague feeling of disappointment to what Spadger Peck had recalled. She tried not to show this to Spadger, whose memory and local knowledge on all matters related to local farming - even when he was so obviously inebriated – were respected in and beyond the local parishes.

"Well, Spadger, I am really grateful for what you've told me. I have to leave you here and take the path up Priory Lane back home. It's been good talking with you."

"Well, moin'd how yew goo, Miss Smy. Many a one thas jinked their ankle on those rabbit 'oles."

Minutes later, Miss Smy had only just reached the ford when she heard Spadger calling. "Miss Smy, Miss Smy!"

"Yes, Spadger?"

"He wornt a moosician, Miss Smy. I remember it now. He wuz a magician!"

"Ah, Spadger, a magician makes a lot more sense."

*   *   *

As his horse trotted through the small hamlet of Bedingfield, John Stearne once more looked over his shoulder to check that he wasn't being followed. In fact, ever since he'd left Diss, he'd found himself compelled to check that neither Hopkins nor Parsley was stalking him. That morning he had confirmed that he would be taking the road to Bury St Edmunds, calling in on two villages along the way that had petitioned him for his assistance with some troubling diabolical occurrences. But once he had reached Wortham, he'd abruptly turned left, heading eastwards for Eye before retracing his route back towards Kenton.

At the edge of Kenton village, he dismounted, pulled a small flask of water from a pouch hanging from his saddle and refreshed himself. The heat of the day was rising, and the recently deposited cow dung hummed with the sound of attentive flies feasting off their thin, odoriferous crusts.

Stearne felt like a husband who had betrayed his wife for the first time, and now knew it was not to be the last. He and Matthew Hopkins had had their differences, but this act of deceit on his part marked a point of no return. Along the journey that morning he had tried to reason with himself that duplicity must be met with duplicity, but was that true? Had he not encouraged others with the comforting words from the Book of James: 'Resist the devil, and he will flee from you.' But Hopkins, wily and treacherous Hopkins, was a devil from which he knew he could not flee.

Passing along the narrow road through the village, its surface now deeply incised with ruts that had been baked hard by the summer sun, he soon noticed the dreary cottage of Elizabeth Albrey. There was no jeering crowd now, no hysterical clamour for self-righteous satisfaction. The main door of the house hung askew by a single hinge, as if someone had tried to rip it from the rotten jamb that had once supported it. Dark shadows sat ominously behind each of the two small shutterless windows, the house resembling, to Stearne's eye, a sinister skull sitting in a bed of sprawling weeds and bleached grasses.

Unrepentant at what had gone before, he walked on and, as he reached the church, remounted his horse. From his now elevated position, he could see a mound of freshly turned earth which he took to be Minister Geffrey's grave, marked by a wooden cross that sat at an angle, cruelly imitating the vicar's contorted arm. A discarded spade lay close by as if the gravedigger, ashamed of the events that had brought the vicar to his final resting place, had wanted to leave the scene as soon as Geffrey's body had been interred.

"So, this is the lane from the church," Stearne muttered to himself.

Passing a timber-framed farmhouse on his left, he could hear a mother scolding a child and the snorts and grunts of pigs from a rudely fenced pen. Stearne's legs squeezed the flanks of his horse to quicken its step. As Hopkins had predicted, within minutes Stearne drew level with a smaller lane to his right, which he now turned into. Reaching the end of the lane - as Hopkins had instructed him to do - he turned left and could now see the plantation beyond the next field.

Stearne remembered Hopkins' instructions and established the 'mid-point' of the wood's width that he'd first described. Tying his horse to a broken stump, he entered but not before he had one final check that he was truly alone. Nothing but the calls and responses of birds carolled through the surrounding branches. Stearne counted his paces as he entered, finding that –

as Hopkins had assured him – he was able to pursue a straight line some way into the plantation without any impediment.

When he saw the beech, it was almost exactly as he had imagined it in his mind's eye when Hopkins had described what he should find. He rushed and looked at the opposite side of the tree. There it was! There was the cross! He immediately looked at the area beyond the tree but then, to his bitter dismay, eyed a large hole only a yard or so away. At the bottom of the hole lay the very cotton bag that the coins had been presented in when the people of Stowmarket had expressed their mercenary gratitude to the witchfinders. Vainly – for he knew it was empty – he reached in and took out the bag. With an angry jerk it was flung to one side.

Thoughts tumbled wildly through Stearne's brain as he desperately tried to rationalise who might have stolen the money. Then it came to him: didn't Edward Parsley interrupt his and Hopkins' conversation only the night before? How long had he been outside with his ear to the door whilst Hopkins had told Stearne about the money's location?

"Parsley! I will kill you, Parsley! I swear it!"

8

A Policeman's Lot

Winifred Smy concentrated very hard as she carefully echoed with her right hand on the piano the melody that Herbert Tranmer had just played on the lower register of his violin. After some moments, her final chord faded, the last steady note of the violin briefly shimmering before ebbing away. A brief and satisfied silence followed.

It was Winifred Smy who spoke first. "I sense that Mr Dvořák was longing for something, something now quite out of reach, when I hear that larghetto."

"Home, perhaps?" suggested Tranmer, as he placed his violin on an adjoining chair.

"Yes, I believe you're right. There is so much painful yearning in the piece."

"You play very sympathetically, Miss Smy."

"Fiddlesticks, Inspector. I am frighteningly average and you know it." Tranmer flinched as Winifred Smy slammed down the lid of the piano.

"Have I said something wrong?"

"Of course not. I…I have remembered something wrong," she replied with a frustrating evasiveness. "Perhaps you would join me in a small sherry?"

Tranmer observed Miss Smy with a professional eye. He knew not to intrude in her thoughts, but could only guess at what those memories were that had caused such sudden anxieties.

"I wish you wouldn't watch me, Inspector. I am not a museum piece."

"I enjoyed our musical soirée tonight. I apologise for my fumbling with the Bach, earlier. It's been a while."

She handed him a sherry and returned to the piano stool.

"I remember you once told me that you and your wife played second violins. I think your playing very fine. Surely you would have been in the first violins?"

"A policeman's lot is not a happy one, as the song goes. In my profession, I keep ungodly hours and strange company. When Annie and I played in our local orchestra it was, ironically, a rare time to be together. I won't deny that the orchestra leader approached me to climb the musical ladder, so to speak, but then I wouldn't have been able to have sat by my Annie. The temptation - or whatever you might choose to call it - of a higher ranking was no temptation at all."

"That's rather noble, Inspector; I very much applaud your loyalty."

Tranmer waved Miss Smy's sentiment away and sipped at his sherry. "I've said before, I wish you wouldn't keep calling me 'Inspector'. I am not a policeman all the time."

"Ah, another example of why a policeman's lot is not a happy one? Then I will compromise. I shall call you Mr Tranmer. Would that be acceptable?"

"Not really, but I feel that it's as much ground as I am going to secure this evening."

"Mr...Tranmer. If you are sincere about your presence here being a non-official visit, then I would like to talk to you about something in the strictest confidence. If you feel that what I say compromises your professional commitments, then you must tell me immediately."

"Of course."

Miss Smy gathered her thoughts, looking for a suitable point from where to begin. She then proceeded to tell Herbert Tranmer the very same details that she had related to Nigel Manners a few days before. Tranmer listened intently, frowning at certain details but keeping his counsel until she had finished. Eventually, all details having now been related to Tranmer, she looked at him keenly for a response.

Tranmer drained his glass and continued to cogitate about what Miss Smy had said. Then, delicately placing down his glass, he raised his head to indicate that the marshalling of his thoughts was now complete.

"Well, Miss Smy, that is rather an extraordinary tale. And that was why you held up the rope so triumphantly that day. It corroborated, in your eyes, with this woman's account?"

"I rather take exception to caveats such as 'in your eyes', Inspector."

"Mr Tranmer," he cut in with a finger raised in gentle admonition.

"Mr Tranmer. I apologise, but you did question my account in a rather supercilious way. Anyway, there you have it. It is too much of a coincidence that a rope was at the exact spot that my friend identified. And, if I may add one other observation, much of the vegetation had been recently trampled in that particular area, whereas the rest of the undergrowth in that wood had not been disturbed."

"And what do you know about this Mr Pallant? Is he a local man?"

"There's the rub, Mr Tranmer. Not only is he a stranger to this area, but he has purchased parcels of wood between the railway line and Bellwell Lane and I am sure that it was him that was posing as the witchfinder."

"But why a witchfinder? There are two things that seem strange about this. First, why he would want to draw attention to himself - because that is how it appears to me - and why he would wear the attire of a witchfinder?"

"As someone who has recently chosen to reside in Suffolk, you would do well to know a little of the shameful events that have bedevilled this area. Mr Tranmer, even though this county appears a peaceful and contented place, there still lingers the horrific memory of the witch hunts that took place only 250 years ago. You have to understand it is not that we are living in the past, but the folk memory of local innocent women and men executed as witches has not been forgotten."

Tranmer rested his hands on his lap and started to twiddle his thumbs. "It all seems very far-fetched to me. What possible motivation would someone have for buying up some bit of forest and then attempting to openly draw attention to himself by frightening passing train passengers out of their wits?"

"The very questions I have been asking myself. There is one fact that I must add to all this. I have learned since that Mr Pallant is something of a conjurer, a magician. I would imagine that arranging these rather gruesome spectacles might well be in his line."

"Most entertaining, Miss Smy! Your fanciful story has rather rounded off our evening on a lighter note. And even if what you say were true, well the man hasn't broken any law, so I would dismiss such fripperies from your head."

Miss Smy stood up and defiantly slammed the palm of her hand down on the table.

"Don't you ever, ever dismiss my conversation as 'fripperies', Inspector."

"Mr Tranmer."

"No, Inspector! When a woman in our village is deeply unnerved by witnessing such a disturbing vision, I do not call that a frippery. You would do well to remember that a woman has the right to feel safe in her home, in her place of work and as she goes about her daily business. You men are too fond of belittling the valid concerns of my gender with your patronising dismissals. Disagree with my viewpoints - I have no truck with that - but do not so lightly set aside our anxieties and worries."

Tranmer's mouth remained open like an expectant gin trap as he took in the anger of Smy's vitriolic outburst. However, he soon gathered himself and stood up.

"Perhaps I should be going."

"Yes, I rather think you should."

It was an embarrassed and rather crestfallen Herbert Tranmer who walked hurriedly from the kitchen and out into the humid air of the summer evening. Smy remained motionless until he had gone; the confirmation of that came with the unmistakeable smack of the door sounding his departure. She then noticed that he had - in his rush to leave - left his violin on a chair. She picked it up and felt the clean wood of its fragile frame in her hands, her fingers following the fingerboard up to the curve of the scroll. Smy then raised the violin to her face, closed her eyes and pressed its body to her cheek. She could just discern the faint odour of maple.

It was then that she started to cry.

* * *

John Stearne wearily rode into Debenham High Street and, after asking a boy who was guiding a recalcitrant cow along the road where a suitable hostelry might be, directed his horse to The Buck's Head Inn. After stabling his steed, he asked for a small meal to be sent to his room. When he had completed washing himself, he sat at the window watching the passing villagers as they went about their business. A fight between two children had broken out about a game they were playing that seemed to involve several sticks and a hole which they'd scooped out of a small area of dry earth at the roadside edge.

A short succession of firm knocks told him that the food had arrived.

"Come!"

A plate of mutton chops was left on the table, together with a melted Cheshire cheese and a glass of red wine. Stearne surveyed them with disinterest, not really sure if he had the appetite to eat or not. Eventually, he leaned across, took a single chop from the plate and bit into it. It tasted good and he took a peck of salt from a small saucer and seasoned it before taking a second bite.

Having now withdrawn from the rest of his group, sitting in an unfamiliar room overlooking a village street that had the shadows of late afternoon lazily leaning across it, he took stock of his situation. He was almost penniless. That was certain. The villages and towns that summoned himself and Hopkins to deal with their witches were eager to commission them both but frustratingly slow in paying. Again and again, promised sums had not been paid and Stearne - who had foolishly agreed to the suggestion that Hopkins should assume the treasurer role - now found he had precious little money left.

Into these angry deliberations drifted the more benign thoughts of Stearne's wife and children whom he had left behind in Lawshall. The dreariness of his current surroundings necessitated by his itinerant life were in sharp contrast to his much more comfortable existence at home. And for what was he enduring this cheerless existence? At first he and Hopkins had been welcomed with such enthusiasm; villages and towns had been generous in their gifts and he had often found himself assigned to accommodation that was - he felt - entirely befitting his status. But one look at the jaded interior of his present room served to jolt him out of these all-too-pleasant recollections. A box bed sat sullenly in one corner with a mattress thinly stuffed with pea-shucks and straw. The table on which his unfinished meal still sat was splashed from the basin where he had first washed. A gap where the wall and door met told him that his sleep would undoubtedly be interrupted later by the scratchings and scurryings of rodents.

Stearne sighed and reached for his purse. He calculated that Lawshall was perhaps a day's ride away. He had money enough to get home, and there was always the prospect of threatening the villagers of Kenton with the return of their witch if they didn't pay what they now owed him.

And what about the thief, Parsley? The very thought of his name filled Stearne with a sense of violent disgust. Stearne closed his eyes and muttered menacingly, "To me belongeth vengeance and recompense; their foot shall slide in due time: for the day of their calamity is at hand."

9

The Lyons Share

As Winifred Smy entered the Lyons Café at exactly twelve noon, she eagerly eyed the room and its many occupants. The loud aural blur of so many indistinct conversations swelled and ebbed, the general sound occasionally punctured by the chinks of china returning to rest on china, or the stirring of spoons in different combinations of tea, sugar and milk. At one table, the *coup de grâce* of a barbed remark was immediately met with an approval of laughter that soared above the din before rapidly subsiding into the general chatter and gossip that filled the room.

"Have you reserved a table Ma'am?" said the waitress, suddenly appearing above the side table, catching Miss Smy unawares.

"Pardon? Oh no, I am meeting a Mr Pallant. I understand that he has a table already booked for us."

"Yes, Mr Pallant is already here."

This confused Smy and she scanned the entire café once more desperately trying to think who Mr Pallant might be, and then wondered whether there must be an adjoining room in which he might be waiting. Yet, with a brief signal that she should follow, Miss Smy dutifully trailed the waitress and found herself faced with a small, middle-aged and rather dull looking man. He stood and affected a slight bow. He was perhaps in his early 60s, with thin, greying hair that was sparse about the temples, a thin lipped mouth and an aquiline nose that seemed curiously out of place on his head, as if a poor make-up artist had awkwardly placed it there. He smiled and beckoned that Miss Smy should sit opposite him.

"Neighbours, eh?" he enquired as both sat down, his deep and resonant voice instantly noted by those at adjacent tables.

"If parcels of land can be considered dwelling places, then I believe we are."

Pallant sat self-importantly back in his chair, his right arm resting on the top of the backrest. A slight smile could be detected by the small movements of his lips whilst his penetrating green eyes coldly steadied on Miss Smy.

"Are we here to stare or to talk, Mr Pallant. I am so much more inclined to the latter."

"Of course, but do forgive my impertinence. Your face really does have the most fascinating bone structure."

"Poppycock, Mr Pallant. I am not some witless member of your audience. If we are to engage in a fruitful conversation, then it will be one devoid of such inanities. Now, I am going to order some tea. Would you like to join me?"

"Coffee for me, Miss Smy. I find tea a quite insipid beverage."

Mr Pallant folded his newspaper and pushed it to one side. He then rested his chin on both hands, leant forward and coolly regarded Winifred Smy.

"Your Mr Manners is a quite persistent man. Most persistent indeed. He felt that there would be something profitable to us both if we should meet. I rather doubt it, if you will permit some candour on my part. 'Profitable' is a word that I happily associate with revenue, whereas I suspect that Mr Manners' interpretation of the word is more altruistic."

Winifred Smy found herself taking a rapid dislike to Mr Cecil Pallant. She was expecting someone different, someone inscrutable, exciting and fey. But the man across the table was overweight, pasty and even somewhat repellant. She found it very hard to think of him upon a stage performing in front of any large enraptured crowd. He seemed to her more like some tedious Roman governor of an unimportant province at the very edge of its empire.

"I hear some incredible things from the Kenton environs, Miss Smy. Stupendous apparitions of witchfinders and other such magical manifestations. And all on my newly acquired land, would you believe?"

Miss Smy smiled enigmatically and placed her handbag by her chair. As she did so, she noticed that Pallant had placed his black Homburg hat on the opposite empty chair.

"All most mysterious," Pallant continued. "Very mysterious, indeed. Perhaps I need to charge a rent? After all, it's most galling to have an interloper replicate my profession within one's very own newly acquired plantation."

A loud conversation suddenly diverted Miss Smy's attention to the café's entrance. "Tell me, Mr Pallant, is that Edward Ransome, the Ipswich mayor who's just arrived? You can see much better than I can."

Pallant shifted his weight to one side and looked towards the door. "The mayor? I'm not sure...Oh, yes, I believe it is."

"How the mighty are fallen. I would not associate him with afternoon tea in an establishment such as this."

"A man of many talents, I hear. Engineer...artist..."

Miss Smy raised her eyes to those of Pallant's and seized his attention in an instant. Pallant's gaze wavered momentarily and he affected to smooth some strands of loose grey hair behind his ear.

"How much has Mr Manners told you, Mr Pallant?"

"Mr Manners? Oh, enough to intrigue me. Especially as the 'sighting' seems to have been by someone looking at my property from a train."

Winifred Smy narrowed her eyes. "Perhaps it is nothing but the high jinks of some accomplished magician?"

Pallant took offence immediately. "Then you must remove your suspicion of myself immediately. I am an illusionist, not a magician. If it was an illusionist that you would suspect, then I'm your man and you must exercise your powers of a citizen's arrest immediately. Except that, most unfortunately, I am not your man. The fourth-rate manipulation that these magicians use - where mere conjuring masquerades as visual illusion - is not my style."

The waitress appeared at the table with a tray of crockery. "Oh, the coffee is mine, the tea is Miss Smy's." She noticed how

Mr Pallant relayed this information to the waitress whilst looking out of the window in a very self-important manner.

Winifred Smy realised that - contrary to what she expected to believe - she was disconcertingly convinced by Pallant's denial. Rather than challenge or accept his statement, she directed her attention in the pouring of tea, endeavouring to look entirely neutral with regard to Pallant's explanations.

"You're not convinced by what I have just told you, Miss Smy?"

"It is not that I am not convinced, rather that I prefer to retain an open mind on the point."

Pallant snorted and reached for his coffee. "Surely it's the same thing, don't you know?"

Smy looked across the café once more. "I do believe it is Mr Ransome. I've only seen his photograph in the newspaper. It either wasn't a good likeness or a very old photograph."

Mr Pallant quickly felt on surer ground and almost seemed to become taller in his chair. "That is exactly the art I ply! What is a photograph? It is but a distortion of reality. A two-dimensional, limited representation of a human being. When I am performing, my aim is identical to the flattering photographer. Distort the audience's reality so that their concentration is shifted to what you would want them to see. Oh, by the bye, have you seen my act?"

"Before these events, I must confess to having never heard of you. Mr Manners did tell me that your stage name is *The Great Pazuzu*. He also informed me that you have an assistant. Adona?"

"Adina. Apparently, it means 'delicate'. A rather unfortunate stage name in both senses."

"I don't follow."

Cecil Pallant rubbed his hand across the smoothness of his balding head and again looked out of the window. "Then follow no more and leave the matter there. I honestly rue the day I employed her. Of course, Adina is not her real name. But one never knows quite where one is with our dear Martha Ludbrook. She is more the illusionist than I can ever be."

"Ah, Martha…A beauty according to Mr Manners?"

Pallant refused to answer, so Smy thought it best to change the subject. "Tell me, are you an Ipswich man?"

"Not Ipswich, but local to Suffolk. I was brought up south of Bury St. Edmunds. Little place called Lawshall. You probably wouldn't know it."

Miss Smy thought for a while, before responding, "No, I don't think I do. My knowledge of that part of Suffolk is very limited."

"Oh, there's nothing to know about Lawshall, except…"

"Except what, Mr Pallant?"

"Well, that it was where a certain John Stearne's residence was."

"Stearne? Oh, the witchfinder?"

Pallant had a devilish gleam in his eye when he looked at Miss Smy.

"Why, yes. The witchfinder."

*   *   *

How tired you look, thought Stearne, as he met his wife who had come out of their house just as he was handing the reins of his horse to the stable boy. In an effort to disguise his troubled thoughts he opened his arms and smiled warmly.

From his chest he could hear his wife proclaim, "You're early. I was not expecting you for weeks. Look at your clothes. Have you been rolling in the dust?"

Stearne laughed. "It was a long ride and I am all the hungrier for it. Tell me, my sweet, how do you fare? And the children. Where are they?"

"They're out playing. Probably the pond at the back of the church."

"You don't exactly know where the children are?"

Stearne's wife stepped back and playfully slapped his arm. "Don't you dare come back and start finding fault with my mothering, Goodfellow Stearne! Perhaps I might have one or two things to say about you always being an absent Father. Anyway, if I'd have known you were returning so soon, I would have had time to fettle the house."

They hugged and went inside, Stearne pulling off his riding boots as they entered the hall. He could detect that his wife was studying him very closely but tried to act as if all was well.

"So?"

"So what, Goodwife Stearne?"

"So what's wrong?"

Stearne pretended to look confused. "By all that is holy, who said anything was wrong? Can a man not return to his homestead for naught other reason than he wanted to?"

"You are an open book, John Stearne. I will chance upon the right page eventually and learn what it is that troubles you, you old dimber-damber."

"In truth, I have had enough of the accursed demons that rove this county. My energy is spent and all I could think about was you and the children. By God's holy grace I am back in the bosom of my beloved, and heartily well pleased to be so."

Agnes Stearne took her husband's discarded boots and neatly arranged them against the wall. "Did they pay you well, John?"

Unfortunately, she looked up at the very moment that his eyelids awkwardly twitched in response to her question.

"I am to be paid well, but we must bide our time until the sums arrive. It is a most sizeable amount. Why, when we were in Stowmarket…"

"So we must fill our children's bellies on promises?"

"All is in hand. As, my love, your bible will tell you in the book of the Philippians, 'But my God shall supply all your need according to his riches in glory by Christ Jesus'."

His wife regarded him coolly before replying, "'But if any provide not for his own, and specially for those of his own house, he hath denied the faith, and is worse than an infidel.' The book of Timothy, if I am not mistaken?"

Stearne chose not to answer and walked into a neighbouring room, easing himself slowly into a wide chair before covering his eyes with his broad hand. Agnes Stearne leaned against the door frame and looked out through the back window into the garden.

"We struggle, Goodfellow Stearne. I try to put a brave face on it all, but the good Lord tests us most hard. There are many wives who are most profligate in their dealings, but not I. I hold steadfast to all we both believe in. But now, despite my efforts, I am struggling. You said most cheerily when you left, 'O taste and see that the Lord is good: blessed is the man that trusteth in him'. And I did most sincerely trust in Him. But that trust has yet to be repaid."

John Stearne withdrew his hand from his face and said, "But the Lord is good and I will be vindicated. There is a great sum that is coming our way, but until that money arrives we may struggle."

Agnes Stearne looked down and smoothed her skirt. The embarrassment of the conversation hung heavily between them.

"John, I have something I would like to propose, but you will take against it, I am sure."

John Stearne returned his hand to his eyes. He was certain what would follow.

"My mother said when we were first married that if the need was great, that she would offer a loan to us."

Stearne, conscious that the relationship between himself and his mother-in-law had considerably cooled since her offer was first made, chose instead to reply, "Your Mother is most kind, but we have no need yet to draw upon her charity."

"You are the master of this house, and I am but a woman, wanting in the very wisdom that you have in such abundance. I have nothing further to add. I will walk down the road and tell the children you are returned."

When his wife had departed, Stearne slowly rose from his chair and entered his study. Closing the door softly behind him - although no one else was in the house - he reluctantly opened his desk and looked for a suitable quill. Agnes had already cut them ready for immediate use. He smoothed the paper with his left hand and began to write.

10

Adina: Entrance and Exit

When she opened the front door of her cottage, Winifred Smy was met by Herbert Tranmer who stood stiffly before her, like a minor Prussian officer.

"I have come to collect my violin."

Winifred Smy paused for a moment in the doorway before inviting Tranmer to enter. He immediately looked for his violin case and opened it to assure himself that everything was present.

"I am not in the habit of stealing violins, Inspector, or their unimportant accessories."

"Mr Tranmer, if you please. I am here as a human being, not a profession."

"Of course you are, Inspector. Now, I have much to do today. Is there anything else I might assist you with?"

"I don't think so, Mrs Smy. Oh, I understand that you met a certain Mr Cecil Pallant two days ago in Ipswich?"

"*Miss* Smy, and let's not play puerile games. How very watchful the East Suffolk Constabulary appears to be. Why, yes, I do believe I met Mr Pallant. How did you know?"

"Oh, because Mr Manners is as watertight as a colander when he's propping up a public bar."

"From your frosty demeanour I suspect that you are anticipating an apology for what I said last week. I regret that you were offended but so was I. If you have come here expecting an apology, then you will be disappointed."

Tranmer closed the clasps on his violin case and now avoided eye contact. "I was expecting to retrieve my violin, nothing more. Now I will be on my way."

Miss Smy followed Tranmer to her front door, with a faint smile just detectable on her lips.

"I wish you a speedy journey back to Framlingham, Inspector."

"Mr Tranmer. How often must I repeat it?"

"Oh, I'm a slow learner. I look forward to the opportunity of addressing your surname correctly, but it might take me many years. Are you prepared to tolerate me for that long?"

Tranmer was stumped for a reply, and chose instead to awkwardly raise his hat before turning and walking down the garden path. Suddenly, he halted and turned around.

"Am I to take it that you have not heard the news?"

"News? What news?"

"Pallant's assistant, Adina."

"Adina?"

"Adina, or Martha Ludbrook, which was her real name. Murdered yesterday. Stabbed in Ipswich. It's in all the Suffolk papers."

"Adina? But why would anyone want to do such a savage thing?"

"That, my dear Miss Smy, is a matter for the police. I do hope my inference that your involvement is not required will meet with your assent." Tranmer smiled ruefully, raised his hat once more and abruptly left.

Winifred Smy remained at her cottage door, still unable to quite believe what she had heard. The conversation she had so recently had with Pallant came hurriedly back to her, and she desperately tried to untangle the meaningful from the meaningless. What was it he had said when he spoke about his assistant? Her thought interrogated all that she could remember, and then one remark she was able to summon startled her: "I honestly rue the day I employed her... She is more the illusionist than I can ever be."

Was there more to those frustrated asides than she had suspected? When she had been conversing with Pallant and he had looked out of the window, which she noticed him doing on several occasions, were there murderous intentions teeming through his mind?

Smy went back into the house and sat solemnly at the kitchen table. Her initial agitation had been about the sighting of a supposed witchfinder. But now events had taken a darker, more sinister turn. She would have to rethink all that had gone before. The old churchwarden's letter found by the Reverend Pilbeam. The confusing involvement of Nigel Manners. The apparent innocence - as she had perhaps wrongly decided - of Mr Pallant. She realised that she had been flailing around, approaching these matters in a haphazard way that was most unlike her.

Winifred Smy rose from her chair and opened a drawer in the kitchen dresser. Taking a small sheet of paper and a fountain pen, she returned to the table and sat down. In the centre of the blank page she wrote the single word, 'Murder'. Then she wrote, towards the top of the page, 'Mr Cecil Pallant'. With a steady hand, she drew a continuous line from one to the other, before carefully drawing a question mark to one side of it. She then drew a second line that began at Cecil Pallant and continued to an empty space towards the right-hand side of the page. Here she wrote 'witchfinder' and again wrote a question mark against it.

Winfred Smy turned over in her mind what she had just written. Maybe *The Great Pazuzu* was a greater illusionist than Winifred Smy had realised? Was the appearance of the witchfinder in Low Plantation pertinent or merely a coincidence? Coincidence or not, she was certain that one name linked both events, and that name was Mr Cecil Pallant.

She returned to the dresser, drew another sheet of writing paper from the drawer and sat down again at the kitchen table. She smoothed the paper with her left hand and began to write.

Dear Mr Houghton-Gale

I do hope that this letter does not intrude upon your parish duties, but the Reverend Pilbeam, with whom I believe you are well acquainted, suggested I write to you to request...

*   *   *

Stearne's quill hovered for some moments above the paper. He sucked in his cheeks and started to write...

My best beloved Mother-in-Law

I write this letter as one in great difficulty. As you are already aware, I have set aside my own safety and journeyed amongst these adjoining counties with a determination to unmask Lucifer in whichever guises he has masqueraded and to banish both he and his tormentors from us forever. In committing myself to this purpose I have set aside my own needs to pursue those that are aligned with a spirit that is profoundly loftier than mine.

Yet, and I must be candid as I relate this matter to you, this very commitment has involved great personal hardship. In following God's calling, I have realised that the sacrifice extends beyond myself to those that I hold dearest: my deeply beloved wife and family. When I have relentlessly hunted down those that seek to invoke Satan and his works amongst us, I failed to observe that there were sacrifices that those nearest to me were also making as I pursued God's holy commands.

So, against all the noblest desires of my heart, I find myself humbly approaching you to help me in my labours. If I am to continue to succeed in driving out the demonic presence that lurks amongst this portion of Albion, then I truly seek your counsel first and your financial aid next. As for the first, you have been unfailingly generous. With the second you have never stinted to support myself and your daughter, Agnes. Yet, with great humility, I find myself prostrating myself before you once again to plead your continued assistance so that I might continue what the Great Almighty has summoned me to do.

You would rightly ask, 'How are you to pay me back?' This, I will reveal to you and you alone. As recompense for my intercession in their towns and villages, many have wanted to donate their appreciation by making generous monetary gifts to myself and my lowly assistant, Matthew Hopkins. Such have been our labours that, over many months, this financial reward has grown to such an extent that my assistant thought it prudent that we should hide the money for fear of being robbed. I took the decision that this must be our choice and the money now lies in a safe place between two villages in the East of this county: Debenham and Kenton. Indeed, along the tracks that link these two locations is a small plantation of trees owned by a Mr Leucock where we have secreted the monies until the good time that we might safely collect them.

So, as you see, my need for assistance is but a temporary one, and your confidence in me will be repaid manifold. Is it not Matthew who writes, 'Therefore take no thought, saying, What shall we eat? or, What shall we drink? or, Wherewithal shall we be clothed? Knoweth that ye have need of all these things.' Yea, we have need of all these things, but for a very short time until we can collect the fees that we have honestly and rightly deserved.

Perhaps you might permit me one last point on this. Whilst in a church in Rattlesden, I overheard a conversation that revealed that Hopkins, my assistant, had taken ill with consumption and, according to one source, was unlikely to last more than a month. God bless that good man's soul and grant him liberty from such a terrible ordeal. Nevertheless, should he die soonest, then the total sum - which we had previously divided between us - falls entirely to me. I must admit that the fact that we were paid by the the town leaders of Stowmarket with Oxford Crown coin, minted in honour of our treasonous king, troubled me somewhat, but I have set my reservations aside. It remains the coin of our country and I must not be too pernickety as to its provenance.

This letter has already taken up too much of your time and I will therefore hasten to close it. Look kindly on us, my most beloved relation, and know that we would only beseech your kindness in a great hour of need. My fervent wish is that you might look upon this humble request knowing that - when fortune inevitably turns in our favour - we will repay you handsomely in reply.

I have the good fortune to know that Edward Creke means to visit near you this afternoon and it is to him that I will entrust this letter for deliverance.

Your truly devoted Son-in-Law while I breathe,

John Stearne

11

All That Glisters

Winifred Smy took a deep breath and knocked the clapper hard on the door. After a few moments a woman carrying a squealing child, which she did with a single arm, answered.

"Yes?"

"Mrs Houghton-Gale? I'm Winifred Smy. I have an appointment with your husband."

The woman looked confused for a moment. "Really? My husband? He never told me."

Smy looked perplexed and tried to explain. "The Reverend Pilbeam, who assures me that he is a friend of your husband, suggested I send a letter. I have his letter of reply..." But she was interrupted by a voice that erupted from within the house. "Indeed, you're expected. Bring her in, dearest. Miss Smy is most welcome."

The woman at the door withdrew and indicated with a small nod of her head that Smy should enter. "My apologies, my husband is not known for his communication."

"Prithee, enter, good Miss Smy!" came a voice from an adjacent room. "Even the basest Catholics and heretics are welcome in this house!"

The woman with the baby showed no surprise, indicating that she was obviously used to the theatrical behaviour of her husband. Smy entered, placed her handbag and umbrella by the hall table and made for the room from which boomed the dramatic voice.

"Mr Houghton-Gale?"

"An amazing coincidence, for that is my name as well! Pray, make yourself comfortable."

From behind a rather large, heavy oak desk sprang a tall man with a lithe and, at first glance, athletic frame. Smy was astonished by his handsomeness. He had clear blue eyes that instantly brought to her mind the hue of the willow pattern of the one remaining plate of value that she secreted in her dresser. His thick brown hair, smoothed constantly back by his hand, sat above a smooth, intelligent face that was disturbingly attractive to her.

"I must say, you are just as I imagined you, Miss Smy. Mr Pilbeam is quite the admirer of you and I can certainly see why."

Miss Smy bridled at the forwardness of the remark. "But you may have limited imagination, Mr Houghton-Gale."

"Oh, my imagination is completely unfettered, I assure you." He smiled for a moment, enjoying his response to Miss Smy's question before continuing, "But to business. Tiresome I know, but it is the reason for your visit, is it not? Oh, may I get you some tea?"

"That would be most kind of you. It's a rather long journey to this part of Essex."

"Yes, the modern world with its pistons and engines and whatnot rather bypass us here in Layer de la Haye, but the newspapers keep our hick settlement appraised of events national and international."

Winifred Smy coolly regarded him. He was utterly self-confident, and reclined in his chair, sat like a man with the answer for all things. Even his desk, she observed, was organised with papers and writing paraphernalia arranged precisely to hand. How different to dear, bumbling Mr Pilbeam, squat in body and relying on his Pickwickian charm to cover his many shortcomings.

"Yes, it is the reason for my visit. Your good friend and mine, Reverend Pilbeam, has assured me that you have some considerable expertise in the historical artefacts of this county?"

The Reverend Houghton-Gale shook his head dismissively. "He is most generous. No, too generous! I am interested - no, fascinated - in what lies hidden around us. But I would be reluctant to call it 'expertise'."

"And yet Mister Pilbeam was most impressed by your remarks relating to a letter from Mr Mouser, a Suffolk churchwarden from many years ago."

Houghton-Gale leapt from his chair as soon as Miss Smy mentioned Mouser's name. "Why, yes! A most interesting letter. Such a privilege that he should bring it to my attention. Are you related to our good churchwarden, Mr Mouser?"

Winifred Smy chose not to reply directly, and affected to arrange the pleats of her skirt. "I would just like to ask you some questions related to the letter. My interest is purely academic."

Houghton-Gale walked behind Miss Smy, his voice suddenly speaking close to her ear so that she could feel his warm breath on the back of her neck. "Mr Mouser's letter intrigues you? You intrigue me."

"Desist, Mr Houghton-Gale, please!"

Houghton-Gale swept around and returned to his desk chair, seemingly oblivious to Smy's discomfort.

"Mr Mouser's letter has great interest for me. After all, it depicts a murder of an innocent man. Does not that fact trouble you also?"

Houghton-Gale turned his chair to one side, before responding, "Not really."

"Not really?"

"Why, yes. I cannot bring this poor man back to life or visit justice on those that perpetrated this obviously heinous act. So, to be blunt, I am completely untroubled by the whole incident."

Winifred Smy chose to mask her irritation by looking to one side, taking in the long line of poetry books that were contained in Houghton-Gale's impressive bookshelves. "Tell me, what did you make of the letter?"

Houghton-Gale rose from his chair and sat on the corner of his desk, his knee uncomfortably close to Smy's. It was then that she realised that this was a man who, with the good fortune of pleasing looks, was used to forcefully pushing against the walls of impropriety.

"You seem to have a lot of devilish questions, Miss Smy. I'm fascinated - very fascinated - why the rantings of some minor churchwarden should have such a hold on your pretty intellect. Are these questions not better left to more forensic minds?"

"Do you mean male minds, Mr Houghton-Gale?"

He patted her shoulder and returned once more to his chair. It was then that Smy noticed a column of thin drawers to her left. "May I ask what you keep in those drawers? Those drawers just there."

Houghton-Gale once more leapt excitedly from his chair. "Miss Smy, you are a person of discernment, I knew it! You probably have me down for the most frightful cad but there is more to me than meets the eye. This..." and he indicated the area that he wished to draw attention to with a small flourish "...is my lifetime's work. A collection of coins that is the envy of the most august establishments."

"You're a coin collector?"

He stood with his mouth open in astonishment. "A coin collector, good lady? How dare you! I am no mere coin collector; I am a numismatist!"

"Is there a difference? I find you men rather tediously obsessed with semantics. Apparently, according to a very recent conversation, an illusionist takes offence when called a magician. And now it seems that numismatists bridle when referred to as coin collectors."

"We bridle indeed! It is not the mere accumulation of coins of worth, but the intense study of the very history that all those coins carry in the truest sense. My particular passion is for English coin from the 18th century and before. In these drawers

I hold many fine examples from the very earliest times. Let me just show you one."

He took a key that hung on the end of his fob chain, unlocked the master lock and opened one drawer. It revealed a variety of coins - Smy calculated perhaps 20 or more - all neatly arranged in serried ranks on a green baize cloth. Houghton-Gale's hand instantly went to one particular coin which he placed in his left palm and held out for Miss Smy to inspect.

"That, my dear one, is very special. From the reign of Henry III. Minted in the mid-thirteenth century by William of Gloucester. You'll see it is gold, gold imported from the exotic and far-distant lands of Africa. But, aside from that, do you know why it is so special?"

Smy did not bother to answer. With a showy flourish, he turned the coin over.

"Because this," and he pointed to the small image of Henry on the coin. "This is the first portrait of a king upon the English throne since the time of William the Conqueror, no less!"

"It must be an absorbing hobby."

Mr Houghton-Gale snorted with derision at Smy's observation. "Hobby? It is no hobby. It is an obsession. There are coins in here that I have obtained with behaviour that you would find most unbecoming to a man of the cloth. But when I want something, I will have it or no man will have it."

"May I return to Mr Mouser's letter? I am loth to take up so much of your valuable time."

Houghton-Gale instantly resumed his former engaging manner, the rapidity of his mood change rather unnerving her. "Oh, my dearest dear, I do forget myself. *Mea culpa. Mea culpa.* Have mercy on such a poor display of manners. My attention is entirely on you."

"Well…"

"Now where is that tea?" Houghton-Gale walked decidedly to the study door, opened it and hollered, "Harriet! Make haste with that tea or our guest will be forced to return to her home with no refreshment!"

Only a few moments later his servant bustled in with a tray which she hurriedly set down. After making sure that the Reverend Houghton-Gale and his guest were happy with their tea and cakes, she made the smallest of bows - but, as Miss Smy observed, with an easily discernible air of resentment - before withdrawing.

"Now, my delicious Miss Smy. Where were we?"

"Reverend Pilbeam informed me that you corroborated the provenance of Mr Mouser's letter. As I said earlier, he holds your opinion on such matters in high regard."

He acknowledged the praise with a small nod of his head.

"You will know," continued Miss Smy, "that it tells of a visit to my village by two witchfinders and their retinue. I understand that the woman they identified - whom they apparently proved to be a witch - was executed."

"Not so."

"Really?"

"Incarcerated in Colchester Castle. In those times its Norman walls housed the town's gaol. From my own research it was a frightfully filthy place. Our poor Widow Albrey perished before they could execute her. If it wasn't gaol fever that took that good lady's soul, then some other disease or malnutrition robbed the hangman of his day on the gallows."

"How did you find all this out?"

"The archives at the Shire Hall in Chelmsford. There was the most funny little archivist chap there, annoyingly Frenchified if you get my drift, but very helpful nonetheless."

"I am somewhat alarmed by what you said about the lady accused of witchcraft. I regret that we now find parallel events unfolding in our village. You see, someone from the village is certain that they saw the figure of a witchfinder in a nearby wood. They were on the train from Haughley and, as it slowed down to arrive at Kenton Station, she noticed not only the witchfinder whom I have mentioned, but the dreadful sight of a woman hanging from a tree beside him."

The look on Houghton-Gale's face appeared to register a small degree of pleasure, which he seemed to find difficult to contain. "Tell me, are you quite sure of this? I mean, had the woman in question been under some degree of stress or anxiety, perhaps?"

"I can assure you that this woman is not that sort of person, as the Reverend Pilbeam will attest."

"And this sighting. When did it happen?"

"About three weeks ago. It is the talk of the village and has caused a great deal of worry and consternation. There is one other occurrence that I must add."

"Please, this is most compelling."

"Some time ago, a Mr Cecil Pallant purchased three parcels of woodland in the area. It was in one of these small copses that the witchfinder was seen."

"I'm sorry, I can't quite see the connection."

"I have learned he is an illusionist of some renown; his stage name is *The Great Pazuzu.* Although he is usually resident in Ipswich, his act has earned him the most favourable notices right across the country. In his employ was a woman who assisted him on the stage. Although she was always known to audiences as 'Adina', her real name was Martha Ludbrook."

Houghton-Gale leaned forward with interest. "You say 'was'. Has something happened to her?"

"I regret to say she was murdered only a few days ago, the 25th of June to be exact, in Ipswich. Stabbed to death in the street."

Houghton-Gale stared hard at his desk and it was some moments before he asked in a lower voice, "Tell me, Miss Smy, how many people know about this sighting?"

"I would say all of East Suffolk, by now. You see, the dreadful witchfinder events - even though they happened such a long time ago - feed a thousand impressionable minds. I regret that we Suffolkers can be a superstitious people."

Smy could just detect a 'damn' angrily uttered by the lips of Houghton-Gale. The self-confidence and broad theatricality of his manner had now quite vanished. Why did the information - especially that relating to the sighting of the Witchfinder - seem to shake him so deeply? She finished what remained of her tea and rose to leave.

"Thank you for your time, Mr Houghton-Gale. Do you know that your wrist is bleeding? I noticed it when you showed me the coin."

"Oh, oh that. I caught my hand on several nails that were on a broken fence. It's nothing really."

"I enjoyed seeing your coins. Tell me, have you ever fallen for a forgery?"

"Oh no, they are fairly easy to spot. All that glitters is not gold, eh?"

"I think Shakespeare actually wrote 'glisters', but the old saw still works whichever way you say it. The saying does have a certain resonance with all I'm involved in at the moment. It seems to me that events - and people - are not quite what they seem."

*   *   *

"You don't look well, master. Not well at all."

Hopkins ignored Edward Parsley but continued checking over his horse, smoothing his hand along its shining flank.

"Is she ready?"

"She's good. Just brushed her down and she's 'appy enough."

Satisfied, Hopkins stepped back and flicked a piece of straw from his trousers.

"That priest, Mr Parsley..."

Parsley, always visibly uncomfortable when conversation veered away from animals or the bible, conveniently turned away to make sure that the stable door was firmly pushed open.

"And which priest is that, Mr 'opkins?"

"You know the priest I'm referring to. The Kenton Priest. Geffrey. Minister Geffrey. What do you know about him?"

An uncomfortable Parsley eventually answered, "The Kenton Priest? 'E weren't a priest. Not a real one."

"What do you mean?"

Parsley kept his eyes averted, "Any man - priest or not - that prevents your good work is in the devil's pay. That's what I think and no one will tell me otherwise."

"Mr Parsley, please speak the truth for I must ask you a difficult question."

"I always speak the truth. Before you and before God. You know that, sir."

Hopkins drew up alongside Parsley until both men were looking out onto the small courtyard.

"What do you know of Mr Geffrey's demise, Edward? Speak plainly to me. I ask not in judgement, but out of merest curiosity."

"He was shadderin' yer."

"Shadowing me? What do you mean?"

"That evening when we was first in Kenton, and I'd left that witch with the searchers, I decided to go for a walk. You'd just been speakin' to Master Stearne, I think. You walked back down towards the church and I thought I'd catch up with you and per'aps take the air with you. But just as you went down that little lane that goes past the church, I noticed the priest come out of the church gate. He saw yer, looked around a bit and then started to foller. You didn't see 'im but I did. So bent on watching you 'e were, 'e didn't notice me behind 'im."

Hopkins grimaced as Parsley's tale unfolded. "Go on," he said.

"Well, I saw 'ow upset he was with yer that very mornin'; 'ow upset 'e was with all of us, and I didn't trust 'im. So I crept up along behind 'im. There was a bend in the road, not too far dahn, and I crept up on 'im and put my 'and over 'is mouth and wrestled 'im to the ground. But 'e wouldn't lie still an' I panicked an' 'it 'im to shut 'im up. But I didn't know my own strength and…"

"You killed him?"

"I didn't mean to, Mr 'opkins! I just wanted 'im out the way. We 'ad work to do 'an 'e was vexin' me so much, but I didn't mean to kill 'im!"

"So you made it look like an accident?"

Parsley crouched down and sat on his haunches, staring at the ground. "I ain't a murderer, but when a man gets in the way of God's work an' your work…"

"You smashed his head in with a stone and laid him out by the church tower to make it look like there'd been an accident?"

Parsley's head fell forward and he pulled his foetal crouch into a tighter ball. "What will you do Mr 'opkins? I was only tryin' to protect yer."

"Tell me, Edward, did you follow me afterwards?"

Parsley shook his head and Hopkins discreetly breathed a sigh of relief.

"No, Master 'opkins. I dragged the body into an 'edge and tried to think what to do next."

Hopkins returned to his horse and led it out into the inn's courtyard, before mounting it with the easy grace of an experienced horseman. Except for a passing horse and cart making its way towards the large church at the end of the street, all - save for the excited chirruping of some busying sparrows - was quiet in Diss.

"You commented on my health, Mr Parsley. You are right, I am not well. Not well at all. And, to be honest with you, every day becomes a greater burden. The fierce energy I once had will not return. I know it. I know it because I know that my time is short and, like poor Mister Geffrey, this pleasant summer may well be my last. God will judge me and God will judge you. We have spoken to each other with great candour, and this conversation must not pass to the ears of anyone else. Are we in agreement?"

Parsley rose to his full height, but with his gaze resolutely fixed on the recently swept floor of the stable. "You 'ave my word as I 'ave yours."

"My intention is to go north. I will send a message for you and the searchers when I need you. I have paid the innkeeper for your residence for two further nights."

Hopkins urged his horse on, dipping forward so as to pass safely under the arched entrance to the coaching inn. He then stopped as he reached the road before looking back at Parsley, his eyes narrowed in scrutiny.

"I mean what I say, Mr Parsley. Not a word to anybody."

"Not a word, master."

"A very good day to you, Sir!" he shouted before riding away.

12

No Free Lunch for Mr Manners

The ceaseless drone of so many bees, dancing in the warm air as they passed from flower to flower, was beginning to lull Miss Smy into a pleasant sleep. She was sitting on a bench that faced the large green that spread to one side of Framlingham castle, its formidable yet crumbling walls overtopped with the many branches of ivy that had rooted themselves in its nooks and crannies.

That early July morning, she had left a message at the small and rather dilapidated office of the *Framlingham Weekly News* asking whether, should he have the time, Mr Nigel Manners might care to share some lunch around one 'o clock. Sure enough, as the town clocks were idling towards that very hour, the unmistakable figure of Mr Manners emerged on to the green, his limbs resembling the connecting rods of the wheel of a train that had lost all rhythmic cohesion. His obvious awkwardness was noticed by others walking in the sunshine and occasioned conspiratorial smiles, all of which Mr Manners was entirely unaware of.

"This is my lucky day, Miss Smy. My lucky day, indeed! My rather insipid lunch has gladly given way to your kind offer and I am all a tremble to know what fine fare you have brought with you."

"Your expectations are in great danger of exceeding my simple lunch, Mr Manners, so please do temper those expectations immediately."

"That I will not do. Tell me, have you brought any more of that delicious cake? Oh, tell me you have. It was ambrosia stolen from the Greek gods, I swear."

"I have that cake, but I thought you might prefer to start with a simple sandwich."

Manners' face clouded somewhat, "Do your sandwiches house any pernicious vegetables? I am convinced that man is not meant to consume the limp and the green. I am with the good Doctor Johnson in that, like the cucumber, they should be immediately thrown out of the window."

Smy laughed, "Then you must remove what you cannot bring yourself to eat. I will not take offence. Here," she passed a sandwich that had been neatly quartered. "Start with this."

After extracting pieces of tomato and lettuce, Manners greedily fell to eating, taking the time to look across the green at the ruins of the castle walls. After the first sandwich was despatched, he jerked his head to look at Miss Smy, who was serenely leaning back on the bench with her arm across her open wicker basket.

"Are you not eating?"

"No," Smy lazily replied. "I suddenly find I am not hungry. Perhaps, you will have my share too?"

"Rather! Miss Smy, if you ever do consider taking a husband, would you consider my own meagre qualities? Although I must admit that any man who is fortunate enough to share a domestic bliss with you would soon be of Falstaffian girth."

"I have no desire to make any sort of union with any sort of man. So all the good girths of this county, male and female, are forever safe."

The relish with which the food was eaten was evident in every facial movement of Manners. When he had moved on to his fifth sandwich, Winifred Smy chose that very moment to casually throw out, "I have had the most interesting conversations of late. Conversations that have made me a little uncomfortable, and I could think of no one better than you to share my confidences with."

"Come, come. I am a newspaper man as you well know. Our *modus operandi* is to seek the confidence of others and then brutally betray them. It's an occupational hazard but one that is carried out in the service of our faithful readers."

"I am well acquainted with the limits of your discretion. But you are also a shrewd man who will not forsake a greater prize for a minor one." She withdrew a cake from her basket and passed it to an appreciative Manners.

"True, true. Some stories are - I would imagine - like making a cake. They have a habit of falling flat if withdrawn from the heat before they are fully baked. But I make no promises! I say that to you out of the greatest respect, believe me."

"Let me take my chances. First, you kindly set up a meeting between myself and Mr Pallant."

"Ah, *The Great Pazuzu.*"

"I am very grateful to you for arranging it. It was revealing in a way I did not expect. To be honest, for one who pursues a life in the gay theatres of the land, he seemed a rather dull man to me."

"You were expecting someone a little more, shall we say, flamboyant?"

"Well, yes. Mr Manners, how did you come to know him?" She passed him another slice.

"I must confess to being an *habitué* of the lower forms of entertainment, Miss Smy. I'm sure that a person of your sensibilities is undoubtedly shocked by my admission. In recent times my editor has sent me to various thespian whatnots, but they are either a trifle dull or very dull. But give me the cheaper forms of entertainment and I am boyishly enthralled. That was why, some years ago, I gently persuaded our Mr Pallant to grant me an interview."

"Gently persuaded?" interjected Miss Smy. "I imagine such subtlety is not in your line. Knowing you as I now do, I'm sure he was probably bludgeoned into submission."

"Most unkind, if I may say so, but - I must concede - probably true. It has been a relationship I have been keen to nurture and he also. After all, his constantly favourable notices in this county are often arranged, shall we say, by my enthusiastic influence."

"To be frank, I wanted you to accommodate our meeting because he seemed the most likely candidate for this apparition of the witchfinder. Not only is his trade the creation of illusions, but he had an assistant as well and I was sure that the 'supposed hanging woman' was…"

"Adina?"

"Adina."

"But now you're not so sure?"

Smy raised her eyebrows to signify that she could not decide.

"And then, Miss Smy, Adina is murdered, which muddies the waters even more."

"Exactly. Why would anyone want to do such a thing? Although I did detect a degree of friction towards Adina on the part of Mr Pallant. But is that any reason to murder her?"

"You're right about the discord that was between them. I had the good fortune to meet Adina, and there was no love lost between her and Pallant. You would watch them on stage and it was like viewing the inner workings of a fine watch. But the moment they came offstage the animosity was evident to all."

"Might she have been blackmailing him, Mr Manners? Perhaps it was Pallant and Adina that were seen from the train that day and she spotted a chance to extract a payment for keeping Pallant's stunt to herself?"

Manners grew serious (even though there were flecks of cake still around his mouth) before slowly shaking his head. "I don't know. It's convenient of course to think it could have been Pallant and Adina, but I'm still unconvinced."

"Me too. And then there was yesterday."

"What happened yesterday?"

"I met a Mr Houghton-Gale. The Reverend Pilbeam introduced us."

"Hmm, I don't think I know Mr Houghton-Gale. A local man?"

"Only if you call a small village outside Colchester 'local'. You remember my telling you about that letter Mr Pilbeam found? The one that was discovered in the church during the restoration."

"Vaguely," said Manners, wiping the crumbs from his face of which he'd suddenly become aware. "Churchwarden. Wrote something about his vicar being murdered."

"That's the one. Well, I paid Mr Houghton-Gale a visit. I'm not really sure why. Oh, I asked Mr Pilbeam if I might approach Houghton-Gale. Told him I wanted to ask his colleague more questions about the letter - I was very impressed by all he was able to say about it - but I had some strange intimation that it might throw something else up as well. And it did."

Manners crossed his legs and leaned towards Smy, intrigued by her mysterious smile. "Please tell me, I am sensing scandal."

"Oh, I can't be absolutely certain, but when I told him about the death of Adina, he behaved rather strangely. Yes, the news seemed to exert a greater shock than I could have imagined. I'm sure he knew her. In fact, I am certain he did."

"I see. My journalistic senses are twitching, Miss Smy. Was that all you obtained from your visit, that you suspected he knew the murdered assistant?"

"Oh yes," she responded, now flicking away the bread and cake crumbs from the bench, "except for him letting me see some old coins in his collection. He is quite the collector, apparently. Or quite the numismatist, as he would insist if he were here."

"Let me go back a bit. You said that this man you met…what was his name?"

"The Reverend Houghton-Gale."

"Houghton-Gale, that's the one. You said you suspect that he knew Adina. So, am I to take it that this lovely repast is an advance payment for seeing what I could find out? Whether the two are connected or not?"

"Well, yes, that would be most helpful. But that is not the main reason I wanted to talk to you today."

Manners sat up, his hand suddenly brought up to his face as if to cover his awkwardness.

"I feel outmanoeuvred here, Miss Smy, and rather uneasy with it, I admit. Like when a policeman pulls me over on my bicycle even though I am certain I have done nothing wrong."

"You know more about this witchfinder sighting than you're letting on, don't you?"

Again, the twitch of a leg immediately betrayed Manners' discomfort. "I can't think why you would say that."

"That day we met in the churchyard. Why were you there, Mr Manners? It struck me afterwards that you were seeking me out. Was it really just serendipity that brought you to Kenton that day? Be honest in your response. I have brought you into my confidence, now I expect you to entrust me with what you know."

Manners now slid his thin buttocks forward on the bench and placed his hands between his knees. "Well, I must admit…that is…I was eager to…Oh, dash it, Miss Smy. I was following up on a story! You see, oh I really feel I shouldn't be telling you this. It's quite irregular. In fact, highly irregular."

"Spit it out, Mr Manners."

"Well, your lady…"

"The one who saw the witchfinder?"

"The very same. You see, she wasn't the only one to see him or that hanging woman."

"So someone else saw him as well? Who?"

"Well, it was…if I must be honest…it was me."

*   *   *

Stearne had become increasingly anxious. He'd received no answer to his letter to Mrs Cawston, his Mother-in-Law and, despite his best efforts to disguise his increasing anxiety about his financial situation, he knew his wife was too shrewd not to have noticed. Under the pretence of returning to those villages that had yet to pay him for his labours, he had bid his wife and children goodbye and headed once more into the heart of Suffolk.

He first visited Creeting All Saints where, some years before, he and his searchers had discovered how Nicholas Hempstead had been using his demonic skills to kill horses that had been reared for the parliamentary armies. The sums they had assured him would be paid had yet to appear. However, Samuel Spring, the minister of the village could not be found and Stearne was reminded by the villagers that it was he that had set aside the sums that belonged to him. Stearne, with a promise to the inhabitants that he would return to claim his payment, wearily turned his path towards Kenton.

Although Kenton had, like Creeting All Saints, so far avoided paying the witchfinder, the real reason for his return to that particular village needled like a restless scorpion in his chest. For some reason that he couldn't articulate, he wanted to return to the wood where the money had been stolen by Parsley.

Leaving the Roman Road that linked the minor villages of mid-Suffolk to the great city of Norwich, he stopped at a small village called Pettaugh where a large pond - partly hidden from the road by reeds bending before a soughing wind - allowed his horse to slake its thirst.

As Stearne sat on the bank and watched the ripples drift across the surface of the water, he reflected on his dire situation. He had intelligence and standing and, let it not be forgotten he reasoned, considerable renown for the progress he had made uncovering the covens of demonic activity that polluted the counties of East Anglia. And yet…and yet… He covered his face with his hands and uttered a prayer.

"Glory to you, O Lord, glory to you. Glory to you, who gave me sleep to refresh my weakness and to repay the toils of this weak flesh…"

When Stearne uncovered his face he noticed that tears had dampened the palms of his hands. He rose, wiped his nose upon the sleeve of his jacket before reaching for the reins of his horse. Once out on the lane again, he calculated where the road to Debenham must lie and rode with renewed energy. Presently, he could see the first rude houses and cottages of Debenham ahead but, seeing a child sitting dreamily upon a grassy bank, he asked where the road lay for Kenton and she pointed to a track that would take him there.

As Stearne approached Kenton, he could feel a slowly rising sense of disgust but, once again, was at a loss to name its source. Was he appalled by his own behaviour? Did the root of his anger lay with Hopkins or Parsley perhaps? Was such disquietude merely the acknowledgement that his life was now reduced to such beggarly circumstances?

Eventually, his horse drew level with All Saints Church, and there still lay the Sexton's spade next to the plot that marked Minister Geffrey's final resting place. As before, he rode past and continued down the small lane that led to the copse he had visited only two weeks before. Again, the noises from the farm cottage to his left indicated that the same pigs were still contentedly scrabbling in the dirt for any roots they could find. Sparrows and finches flew in dizzying patterns between the bushes that lay on either side of the track. The mocking cackle of a Green Woodpecker cut through the loud hum of insects as it fled for cover.

But when Stearne entered the final field and could see the wood that had drawn him with such compulsion, he was alarmed to see that a pony - a pony he instantly recognised - was tethered to the very same tree that he had used when he had previously been there.

He dismounted and, as quietly as he could, settled his horse so that it wouldn't make any noise. He went back to the previous corner and made sure that it was tied up out of sight of anyone who might be in the wood. Then he walked softly along the field path, nearing the entrance to the very copse he had investigated so recently. A close inspection of the pony that was patiently grinding the grass that lay by the entrance to the plantation confirmed his suspicions.

It was Edward Parsley's pony.

13

A Cruel Blow

"You, Mr Manners? You were on the same train?"

"'Fraid so. And now you think I'm an utter cad."

"Oh no, Mr Manners, I think you much worse than that. You came into my house and pretended that what I related that day was completely new to you, when all the time…"

Manners held up his hands in acknowledgement, not sure whether he was deflecting Miss Smy's anger or the potential threat of real physical harm.

"Hear me out, please hear me out!"

"I will not hear you out! You lying, deceitful…"

Smy sprang from the bench, immediately snatched up the lunch basket and strode away. Manners, with gangling limbs, followed for some yards before realising that he had left his hat where they had been sitting and ran back to retrieve it. He then ventured to catch up with a purposeful Winifred Smy who was hastily walking away across the castle green.

"Miss Smy, please, Miss Smy! You have to let me explain!"

"You come to my house, you eat my cake, and then you lie to me under my own roof," Smy threw back. " You are the most unprincipled, mendacious individual I have ever had the misfortune to deal with, Mr Nigel Manners."

"Steady on, Miss Smy, surely even the guilty have the chance to say something before sentence is passed."

"If I thought that you were about to be hung, drawn and quartered - which, believe me, is no less than you deserve - then I would still not give you one more moment of my precious time."

"You see, you see, Miss Smy, I couldn't be sure. I thought I was seeing things."

Miss Smy stopped and rounded on him. "You couldn't be sure? Not sure about seeing some poor woman hanging from a tree? Not sure about someone dressed up as a witchfinder calmly watching your train go past? You really are the end, Mr Manners. The most miserable end!"

"But I was drunk!"

"Drunk? You were drunk?"

Manners, completely crestfallen, closed his eyes in shame. "I'm afraid so. You see, I'd met up with some old chums from my *Ipswich Star* days. I'm afraid I'm not very good with alcohol and I kept company with those who are. The lunch, such as it was, was much more bibulous than I had expected and I was supposed to be seeing my Great Aunt Effie in Stradbroke. That's why I was on the train."

"I didn't know you had a great Aunt Effie?"

"Well, why would you?"

Winifred Smy looked keenly at Manners, still panting from his physical exertions as well as the mental fatigue of his confession. She then swung her basket viciously to the side of Manners' head, causing him to shriek in pain and fall heavily to the ground. Smy then stormed away but called back, "It was the morning train, Mr Manners. You're even more contemptible than I thought."

"I know it was! I was suffering from the worst hangover imaginable! I truly was. I had to get off at Mendlesham and…"

"Spare me the lurid details, Manners. I hope you nearly choked on your own nausea."

Despite his pain, and the unwanted attentions and sniggerings of those who were strolling around the castle grounds, Manners pulled himself upright and ran quickly after Winifred Smy once more.

"You see, I wanted to be sure. And when I heard that someone else had seen the same thing, I thought you would know what had happened."

"So why did you lie to me?"

"Oh, I certainly didn't mean to, Miss Smy. But you were so persuasive with your baking that I didn't have the heart to…well, to own up."

"You seem to have cut your temple. Here. Let me have a look at it."

Smy took a handkerchief from her sleeve and dabbed the blood from Manners' head.

"Mr Manners, do not ever lie to me again. Do we understand each other?"

Manners nodded sheepishly. "I did try to explain my reasons, Miss Smy."

"Believe me, if my blow to your head was in proportion to my level of anger, you would be hanging from the castle turret at this very moment."

Manners turned his head towards Framlingham Castle, as if Smy's warning may have been a valid one.

"But," Miss Smy continued, "your offer of finding out more about Mr Houghton-Gale would be most useful."

"I'll see what I can do. It's been a most…unusual lunch, Miss Smy. I think I'd best return to my office."

Smy placed a hand gently on his arm, and asked, "Can I ask you one more question, before you do?"

"Yes, I only hope I have the answer you require."

"If I wanted to find out more about the witchfinders, where would I go?"

"The witchfinders? Well, given that they were both East Anglian men, the archives office in Chelmsford would be the best place to start."

"In Shire Hall? Of course, that's exactly the place Mr Houghton-Gale suggested. It was where he found out about where the poor woman from Kenton was imprisoned. Apparently she died before they could put her on trial."

"Thurston Hessett is the man you'll want. Very efficient man. Knows his stuff."

"Do you know, I regret what I did just now."

"Oh, I suppose I deserved it a little bit."

"Oh no, Mr Manners. I regret I didn't hit you much, much harder. Good day."

*　　*　　*

From inside the copse there emerged only a cacophony of birdsong. Stearne peered intently into the bracken and grasses from which rose a dense myriad of trees of varying sizes, knowing that within that coarse vegetation Parsley must be present. He waited some minutes to see if any sounds might emanate from the wood, but still the birds' ceaseless antiphony masked any other sounds that might lie within.

Unable to contain his curiosity any longer he ventured further in and passed the tree that Hopkins had first indicated as the marker for where their money lay. Carefully placing the soles of his boots so that a snapping branch would not reveal his presence, he crept ever deeper amongst the trees.

"Looking for something?" came a voice from behind.

Stearne spun around and was faced by Edward Parsley who had a knife menacingly stretched out in front of him.

"A strange place to meet, Mr Parsley? Why are you holding up a knife? Do you intend to kill me?"

"What are you doing here, Master Stearne? What are you doing in this place?"

Stearne gathered his thoughts and slowly replied, "I wanted to check that the money was safe."

"What money? There ain't no money." With this, Parsley lurched forward and brought the tip of the knife against Stearne's throat.

"Then why are you here? And why are you so aggrieved that I should be here?"

Stearne's mind was racing. There *was* no reason for Parsley to be here. If Parsley had found Hopkins' hiding place and taken the money, why had he returned? Despite knowing that the forward lunge of Parsley's knife would end his existence, Stearne was astonished by the presence of an inner calmness and clarity of thought.

"Mr Parsley, I think we have both been deceived."

Parsley's eyes burned with an intense hatred and Stearne realised what contempt this servant - this searcher - must always have held for himself and Hopkins.

"Deceived, Master Stearne?"

"In the name of Christ, put that knife away. We have both been fools. I admit that I have misjudged you, but you have seriously misjudged me. Worst of all, we have both seriously underestimated that venomous toad, Matthew Hopkins."

Although Parsley's knife withdrew slowly, his seething anger remained. "S'robbed us both, Mr Stearne. I 'pologise for 'larming you. But Mr 'opkins is is the worst sort of sorner. He 'as us all in 'is power."

"Not me, Mr Parsley. Not any more. I must admit that when I first saw the empty purse and the hole behind the tree back there, I thought it was you that had taken it. I now know that I have wronged you. After all, if you had that money then you wouldn't be here."

Parsley withdrew his knife and eased it under his belt. "'Nah, I et sech a fool as to believe what that blatherskite tells me."

"Did you find anything?"

"Only that hole back there. Same as you."

"With the empty bag?"

"That bag was always empty. That was 'opkins trick to fool anyone who might look for the money. He deliberately set it up so that if any one of us found it, we would all suspect each uvver. And it worked, didn't it, Master Stearne? You said it yourself, that you thought I'd stolen the money. Nah. The money's 'idden round 'ere somewhere."

"Of course. Why would anyone find the money and throw away the bag. We've been made to look like fools."

"I say we go 'alves. I've worked for 'opkins and yourself for many years, and it's time for 'im to dub up and give me what I'm owed. So 'alves is my offer, Master Stearne, and I won't stand argufying here about it any longer."

"How long have you been here?"

"'Bout 'n 'our."

"Find anything?"

Parsley looked contemptuously at Stearne, "Not yet. But I will. Best get started."

Within the very moment that Parsley had looked down to recover a spade that he'd hidden in the undergrowth, Stearne espied a heavy branch that lay a little distance away. With a swiftness that astonished even him, he reached for the branch and, in the same movement, brought it down heavily on Parsley's skull. The crack of the branch caused by the single blow was so loud that Stearne froze for a moment in case anyone else might have heard it. But all he could hear was the heavy panting of his own chest and, not content that Parsley was now removed from this world, he repeatedly brought down the thick branch upon his head until it was so bloodied that even those who knew him well, would struggle to make out his features.

Stearne fell to his knees, clasped his hands together and prayed, "For the living know that they shall die: but the dead know not any thing, neither have they any more a reward; for the memory of them is forgotten. Oh yes, Mr Parsley, the memory of them is forgotten."

Stearne pulled the body to one side and, seeing a small area that was hidden by a large, sprawling holly bush, chose that place to bury Parsley's body. After an hour or so had passed, he concluded that the depth he had dug, two feet down or so, was sufficient and hauled Parsley's body into the grave. It struck Stearne that even though the line of the grave was east to west which was consistent with the conventions for churchyards, he so arranged Parsley's corpse that he was upside down and back to front. Deciding that there was something fitting about this misalignment, he started to heap earth upon the body. When the hole was finally filled, he patted down the earth with the back of the spade and covered the site with branches which he'd stripped from neighbouring trees.

He threw the spade down and walked back to his horse for his water flask. The sight of Parsley's pony made him realise that with two beasts tethered outside the plantation, he was drawing attention to the area. He looked outwardly from the copse in both directions. Both field paths were empty. He then looked across the adjacent fields to see if there were any labourers within sight but, to his great relief, none were to be seen.

He re-entered the plantation and hid the spade. He tried not to look at the holly bush that now marked the recent internment of Parsley, but found he could not avoid doing so.

Some hours earlier, for a reason he still couldn't explain to himself, John Stearne had returned to this commonplace copse. Now, inside those very trees, lay a man whom he had slain in cold blood. How quickly his life had unravelled from that heated conversation with Matthew Hopkins in Diss, when he was first told of where their money had been secreted. Events had taken a dizzying turn since that meeting, and now here he was, a vile murderer.

In this wood he had taken one of the Lord's commandments and wilfully disobeyed it. And for what? For a bounty of coins that might now be many miles away. Oh, how wily Hopkins was! Did he know that Parsley was outside the door that night when he had so openly shared the location of the coins they had earned? Had Stearne fallen blindly into the trap that had been set for him and Parsley by Hopkins? Yes, perhaps he had. But Stearne was still convinced of one thing. The money was in this very plantation and, by hell or high water, he was going to have it.

14

Une Lampe est Allumée

When Winifred Smy emerged from Chelmsford Station, it was to be greeted by a rather leaden sky that looked heavy with rain. Thankfully, it was a short walk, perhaps two or three minutes or so, from the Station to the Shire Hall and she hurried along the pavement. Once she had entered the building, the first person that Winifred Smy asked was not even aware that there was an archive in the building. The second person, who was coming down the very grand central staircase, was more happily informed and pointed to a nondescript door on the floor above.

Smy knocked on the door, only to be greeted by a bizarre, *"Entrez s'il vous plaît."* She entered and saw to her immediate left a small man behind a large desk, poring over a large map that he had laid out across his desk.

"Puis-je vous aider?" said the man without bothering to look up at Miss Smy.

Unabashed, Miss Smy calmly responded, *"Oui, j'espère. Parlez vous anglais?"*

The man looked up and smiled obsequiously. "Oh, one is a woman?" His curled, tousled hair was receding and lone strands of grey had started to infiltrate themselves within the dark brown loops of his remaining curls.

"One is a woman, and your powers of observation are indeed most impressive. Am I speaking to Mr Hessett?"

"One is a Doctor."

"I beg your pardon?"

"One is Doctor Hessett. Doctor Thurston Hessett."

"Quite. Well, one Doctor Thurston Hessett, I wish to make a request for some files I would like to view. Can you help me?"

Hessett looked irritated, having to abandon his mercatorial studies for someone who was - most alarmingly he thought - not a man.

"Are you sure that one is in the right place? This room is set aside for the study of this county's archives. Perhaps one is in search of something more...more feminine?"

Smy chose not to reply for some moments to allow the heat of her irritation to subside. "Doctor Hessett, do you have any records relating to a Mister John Stearne? I understand that he lived until 1670, by which time he would have been about 60 years of age."

Hessett's eyebrows slowly ascended in a strangely mannered spasm of surprise. "John Stearne, you say? Well, one finds that most interesting. Most interesting, indeed."

"Why so, Doctor Hessett?"

"One has occupied this position since the first opening of these Essex archives. One has, in those five years since, never been troubled to locate the file that relates to Mr Stearne. And now one finds that that very file is requested on several occasions in the last month."

"If you don't mind me asking, by whom?"

Hessett removed his glasses and sat back in his chair. "To one's knowledge, three gentlemen."

"Three gentlemen?"

"Three gentlemen, no less."

"May I ask who they were?"

"One has the sort of mind that finds the retention of details - names, and so forth - quite easy to recall. But one fears that it would be improper to divulge such personal details to one whom one has not had the pleasure of meeting before. I'm sure you'll agree?"

Smy smiled whilst trying to conceal her disappointment. "But perhaps you might compromise such noble ideals and tell me their occupation? You see, I have called upon your office for some rather superficial information. But when other unknown people take an interest in one's kin, one is naturally curious as to from where in society they have hailed from."

"You speak with the wit and wisdom of a man, if I may say so! But one cannot be too cavalier about these matters and one's integrity is too precious a thing to play conversational poker with. Yes, let one see if one can recall their paths of life, so to speak. Why yes, the first was a journalist. A tiresome fellow who shifted constantly in his seat, to the most tedious extent.

Quite wearing when one has to share the same small office with such an ungainly individual."

Smy wanted to smile but retained her neutral demeanour, even though she had no problem with guessing to whom Doctor Hessett was referring. "And the second?"

"Devilishly nice chap. Vicar, don't you know. One must say that one was most deeply impressed by his erudite and, if I may be permitted to add, invigorating conversation. *Il avait une intelligence formidable, Madame.*"

"*Mademoiselle.*"

"Really? How…unorthodox."

"And the third gentleman?"

"Oh, him! Well, one must say he was rather an embarrassment to accommodate, but these are the times one lives in, aren't they?"

"You didn't tell me the third man's profession, Doctor Hessett."

"Didn't I? Oh, perhaps one didn't. A conjurer, magician or whatever. Frightful man, whatever he did."

"A magician? Who'd have thought such a man would be interested in the history of someone who lived so many years ago?"

"Hmm. One is constantly surprised by such encounters. Now, to work, my dear. You need the Stearne files, if one remembers correctly. *Asseyez-vous s'il vous plaît* and one will return with them *très rapidement.*"

Smy pulled back a chair and sat down at a large oak table. So, Manners, Houghton-Gale and Pallant had all requested the Stearne file. Why? What was it that had piqued their interest to such a degree that they had carried out - to satisfy their own individual lines of curiosity - their studies. She was certain that, within that triumvirate, the lynchpin to the whole mystery was hidden. Not only the death of Adina, but the answer to the enigma of the witchfinder sighting.

Hessett bustled back into the room, *"Voici les documents demandés."*

"Merci, Monsieur Hesset, je vous remercie beaucoup."

Smy placed down her bag by the chair and looked at the two large files he had presented to her. A glance towards Dr Hessett revealed him to be once more thoroughly absorbed in his map. She pushed one of the files to the side of the table and opened the other. It contained various documents: a map of Lawshall showing a number of fields, each marked with a different colour; lists of repairs to Stearne's home itemising work carried out and their associated costs; letters to and from tradespeople for sundry goods including a flitch of meat, milk, butter and bread. Smy searched through the entire contents and then closed the file.

She reached for the second file and drew it towards her. As she opened it a voice over her shoulder cut in, "Has one found anything of interest?"

Smy turned to see Hessett smiling benevolently at her.

"It is very interesting indeed, but all rather above me, I'm afraid. Still, I won't be much longer."

"Oh, s'il vous plait prenez votre temps."

"Merci, beaucoup."

Unnerved by his sudden appearance at her table, Miss Smy watched Thurston Hessett soundlessly return to his desk. Then she resumed her inspection of the second folder's contents. Once more, it contained various letters and a set of small black and white photographs of a large cottage, each print carrying the date of 1903 on the back, which Smy assumed to be his residence in Lawshall.

The final set of documents was housed within a buff-coloured paper folder, with a piece of green string tied to contain its contents. She undid the string and was faced with another batch of petty correspondence. Her heart sank and she considered giving up on the task. Then she espied two letters folded together and which seemed different to the bills and letters she had wearily sorted through.

She carefully pulled the letters out and unfolded them; the documents seemed related. One was a letter, dated June 1647 and addressed to Stearne's mother-in-law. It began, *'My best beloved Mother-in-Law - I write this letter as one in great difficulty. As you are already aware, I have set aside my own safety and journeyed amongst these adjoining counties...'*

As she read through it, she was astonished to see that it told of money that lay buried in *'a small plantation of trees owned by a Mr Leucock'*. Smy knew that this plantation was one of the three that Pallant had recently purchased. Her mind became dizzy as she thought through the ramifications of what she was reading. Money in Leucock's Plantation? The plantation still carried his name although the fate of whomever Leucock himself had been was long lost to history. Was there really a small treasure secreted within a small wood she had walked through so often when visiting her friends in Aspall?

She was so taken aback by this first letter that she had almost forgotten about the one that accompanied it. Laying it before her, she soon realised that it was a reply from Stearne's mother-in-law. Peering closely at the ink, which had faded a good deal over the intervening centuries, she read…

My dearest Son-in-Law

I acknowledge receipt of your most curious letter.

Not so many years past, you assured my dear departed husband that, if Agnes was to marry you, she would enjoy a security that few other men could offer. You also communicated to him that, as a man of religious integrity and - in your very own words - a fierce observer of God's laws, you would stand surety for her continued happiness in the great glow of His love.

Yet what does your letter tell me? It tells me that you are embroiled in a most reprehensible situation where your future happiness is dependent upon the death of a colleague and the dubious promise of some few coins that he has squirrelled away like a common thief.

I think it due time that you interrogated your conscience and sought God's intercession so that you might desist from the unspeakable and unseemly life that you now find yourself living.

It was a dark day when you were granted permission by my husband to marry our daughter, but I was permitted no say or could proffer no advice to dissuade him otherwise. I do not intend to compound the original error we made in welcoming you into our lives by granting you the monetary assistance that you now seek. To do so, to my mind, would only sustain the incompatibility of your situation.

I pray that you will one day walk as a child of the light, and flee and shun the works of darkness. I also pray that you will place your faith in the Prince of those who yearn to be led.

Give me leave to return my deepest affection for my daughter and your children.

Mrs Margaret Cawston

Miss Smy slowly refolded the last letter inside the first, so that it was just as she had found it. She then gathered the two large files together and pushed them to the centre of the desk. Outside, the heavy clouds had started to clear and a sharp path of brittle sunshine connected the heavens with the small streets of Chelmsford. And deep within Miss Winifred Smy's fabulous brain, small lamps of insight and understanding were now slowly being lit.

"Doctor Hessett, may I request one more file? That is, if you have such a file."

*   *   *

Stearne was exhausted. He'd studied every inch of the plantation for earth which had recently been turned over, but was disappointed wherever he looked. He sat down and looked again at the empty hole that he had first found, and bitterly accepted that Hopkins had outwitted him. Behind the holly bush lay the recently slaughtered corpse of Edward Parsley. Ahead of him was the realisation that he would be seen as a diminished man. His hour had passed. In a few short weeks his star had fallen spectacularly.

High beyond the trees, he could hear the almost human mew of a buzzard, wheeling above the fields, waiting for the telltale twitch of grass that would reveal its next meal. Stearne had been brought to a depth that he had previously thought the exclusive dominion of the lowly and poor. And now, here he was, not only financially broken, but the most contemptible of murderers as well. In his anger, he blamed the malign workings of Satan and how he had unwittingly been at the mercy of events beyond his control, but he read this thought for what it really was: a vain attempt to step away from any responsibility.

After disposing of Parsley's spade, he emerged again onto the path outside the wood and took up the reins of the dead man's pony, leading it up to where he had hidden his own horse further along the field path towards Kenton village.

When he reached All Saints Church, he tethered his horse and Parsley's pony and walked to the place where he had first seen Geffrey's body. Hanging his head, he closed his eyes and prayed: "Who is like you, Jesus, sweet Jesus? You are the light of those who are spiritually lost. You are the life of those who are spiritually dead."

Opening his eyes he noticed a pinkish stone that lay a little way back from the side wall of the south porch. He rolled it back towards the wall and stared at its new setting. A surge of self-disgust rose within him: salvation was lost. There are pitifully few murderers, he realised, that obtain the blessed dominion of heaven.

15

Careful Arrangements

The force of the collision knocked Tranmer's hat clean off his head and he reeled backward, arms flailing in an effort to at least stay on his feet. "What the damnation..."

"Oh, I"m dreadfully sorry, I just didn't see you. Why, it's you, Mr Tranmer."

Tranmer, looking up and seeing Winifred Smy standing astride her bicycle, couldn't think what to say, except a very pathetic, "Yes, it's me, Miss Smy."

"I was momentarily distracted and wasn't looking at all where I was going. It's my fault entirely. Framlingham is such a busy place." She propped her bike up against the wall and inspected Tranmer's face. "No bruises. Will you live? Oh yes, I think you'll live."

"Whatever were you doing? What do you mean you were distracted? I'm six feet tall, Miss Smy. How can you not see a six foot tall man..."

"A scatterbrain. That's what I am, and no mistake."

Tranmer looked unconvinced. "There is no scatter in your brain. Do you know, I wouldn't be surprised..."

"Your hat, Inspector! It's blowing away!"

Tranmer turned and saw his hat being ushered down Bridge Street by the wind. He ran after it, asking people to excuse him as he pushed through and caught up with it before returning it to his head.

Winifred Smy sat on the wall next to her bicycle with her face turned up to catch the warmth of the sun, shading her eyes with her hand. "Ah, you appear to have rescued it."

Tranmer's hand involuntarily moved towards his hat as if he needed to confirm that he had, indeed, regained it. He looked sternly at Miss Smy. "There are laws that clearly state..."

"Oh yes, I'm sure there are, and if your intention is to berate me with them then I will have to decline your kind offer of my accompanying you around St Michael's Churchyard."

"I don't remember..."

"You don't remember? Oh, that makes it all the worse, but I am quite prepared to let the matter rest. And thank you, the answer is yes."

"The answer is yes to what?"

"To your insistent request that you be allowed to push my bicycle up the hill."

Tranmer rolled his eyes, walked over and, taking the bicycle from the wall, began to push it uphill. Miss Smy walked beside him looking around at nothing in particular.

"Miss Smy, I am trying to be charitable enough to think that what has just happened was a genuine accident, but rather suspect that it wasn't. If it wasn't, then I am led to wonder what possible motive you might have for making it appear as if it was an accident. And then I suddenly recall that yesterday's newspapers announced the arrest of Mr Cecil Pallant for the murder of Martha Ludbrook." He glanced at her to see if his words were having any effect but Miss Smy continued to look blankly around her.

"And," Tranmer continued, "as you are now walking with me as if the recent argument we had counts for nothing, I can only conclude that you are now accompanying me for the sole purpose of extracting information that satisfies some entirely new and fictitious notion of yours."

"Please give me back my bicycle this instant!"

"Tell me if I'm right first, then you can have your bicycle."

"I refuse to answer that question. Now let us carry on to the churchyard where, in the privacy of God's acre, we will be able to talk openly."

"Talk openly about what?"

"The murder of Adina, of course. Mind that cart when you cross." Miss Smy strode ahead whilst an exasperated Tranmer, still pushing the bicycle, followed dutifully behind.

Smy waited at the church gates until Tranmer reached her, indicating to him the place on the inside of the churchyard wall where he should lean the bicycle. They then both ambled along the path that led towards the south porch of the large church of St. Michael's.

"Inspector…"

"Mr Tranmer."

"Ah, yes. Mr Tranmer. I perhaps overreacted the other evening. But what you said rather incensed me."

"That does seem to be a habit of mine when we are in each other's company. But if I say something wrong, then give me an opportunity to correct what I said rather than…well, rather than just humiliating me."

"I will do what I can, Mr Tranmer. I can promise no more."

"So what do you really want to ask me?"

"You'll remember, when you were last at my house, that I told you about the sighting of the witchfinder?"

"No comment."

"Very wise. Well, a visit to a friend of the Reverend Pilbeam's, a Mr Houghton-Gale, was rather instructive and he told me all about what had happened to the Kenton woman they accused of being a witch. Anyway, towards the end of our meeting, I mentioned the murder of Adina and he was quite taken aback. I know that you might dismiss it as just a 'woman's instinct', but I felt sure that he had responded in a way that told me he definitely knew the woman who had been murdered."

"Maybe he was just demonstrating his shock at the news."

"I suspect not, it was somehow too personal. It also contradicted his whole demeanour that he had demonstrated beforehand."

"Demeanour?"

"Oh, believe me, there is something most dislikable about that man. Too fond of himself, too self-assured. A streak of narcissism runs right through him. But when I told him about Martha's death, he changed instantly."

Tranmer removed his hat and looked up at the church. "You know, Miss Smy, in the three or so years I've lived here, I've come to love this church. A very fine chancel. And a splendid organ. Tell me, do you play the organ as well?"

"Oh no, the piano is more than enough for me. It has only three pedals, although I have only ever troubled myself with one of them."

"This Mr Houghton-Gale. Tall chap? Short?"

"Tall. About your size. Slim. Handsome as well, but unfortunately seems very well aware of that fact."

"Then I don't think the police in Ipswich will change their minds about the man they have in custody."

"Ah, yes. As you said, our Mr Pallant has been arrested."

"Tell me, how would you describe Mr Pallant? After all, Mr Manners tells me you both enjoyed a pleasant lunch together."

"We had a very light repast. It wasn't lunch and it wasn't pleasant. Anyway, why are you so sure that it couldn't be someone like Mr Houghton-Gale?"

"Easy enough. According to my Ipswich colleagues, it doesn't match what the witnesses saw."

"Witnesses? There were witnesses?"

"Of course. Apparently she was murdered in Great Colman Street. A short man was seen by several people that night rushing hurriedly past as if to catch up with Martha Ludbrook who was walking some distance ahead."

"What did this man look like?"

"Nobody really caught sight of his face. Well, if you are all travelling in the same direction then you would tend not to notice someone walking past you. Witnesses say he wore a cape

- and bear in mind this is a very warm June evening we are talking about - and his face was screened somewhat by a broad-brimmed hat."

"What time did it happen? The newspaper just says she was murdered in the evening."

"She was murdered at around twenty past ten. The man that was with her had no idea what had happened at first as they had apparently argued and he went on walking ahead. She was stabbed from behind, staggered and fell. By the time that people realised what had happened, the murderer had vanished."

"How did this man stab her?"

"The assailant grabbed her shoulder and the knife entered just below her right shoulder blade."

"You say he was a short man? The man that stabbed her?"

Tranmer gently waved a wasp away from his face. "Absolutely, which is why your Mr Houghton-Gale could not be the perpetrator. The murderer was indeed a small man, which exactly fits with the build of Mr Pallant."

"What about this man's clothes? What was he wearing?"

"Again, a black homburg hat and a red-lined black cape. Perfect for magicians who want to disappear down dark alleys."

"I certainly remember the hat. He kept it on the seat beside him when we first met. What about the man that she was with? What had he noticed?"

"Ah, that we don't know. Apparently, he was walking a little distance ahead and, according to our witnesses, disappeared also."

"Do you think they were acting together?"

"It's hard to say. But instinct tells me probably not. It may well have been that he was somewhere he shouldn't have been, panicked and disappeared. Probably some theatrical type who didn't want to be dragged into it and have his career ruined."

"It's still a curious reaction, him running away like that. Nothing else?"

"No, nothing else. Apart from the fact the murderer was probably religious."

Smy looked confused at Tranmer's remark. "Religious? What made you think the murderer was religious?"

"Oh, because as he brushed past people, he apparently kept repeating, 'Mercy, mercy.' I've often come across criminals with a strangely warped sense of religious justification for their crimes."

"Mercy? Mercy..." Smy smiled serenely at the Inspector. "It was not the language of his faith he was uttering that night, Inspector, *mais la langue du français*."

*   *   *

When the servant opened the door, it was to reveal John Stearne, hat removed, standing a little way back.

"Am I too late?"

"No, Master Stearne. Mr Hopkins is still with us. But it won't be long, I fear."

"I would like to be with him."

The servant opened the door wider and Stearne stepped into the hall. "Has he been bled?"

"Yes, Master Stearne."

"Wintergreen?"

"Of course. You'll see it around the house and in 'is bedroom. But it won't make much difference now. He is closer to the Lord than 'e is to us."

"Alice, he is my greatest friend. Will you leave Mr Hopkins and I alone together? Perhaps, if these are to be his final moments, your master and I might pray together to ease his passage into God's great dominion."

Alice nodded, bowed respectfully and bustled away towards the kitchen. Stearne walked slowly up the long stair and, without knocking, quietly let himself into Hopkins' bedroom. The window to the side had been thrown open, with short gusts of warm wind gently billowing out the curtains. The unmistakable aroma of herbs was immediately apparent as he closed the door softly behind him. Hopkins remained motionless, his body had already wasted away to an alarming degree and his face was covered with a patina of glistening perspiration.

"Matthew. Matthew. Can you hear me?"

Hopkins closed eyelids twitched, and his lips moved strangely as if they were trying to speak some unknown tongue. Stearne could detect Hopkins' breathing quickening, and he put his ear above Hopkins' mouth in case he was trying to tell him something. At last, with awkward movements of his mouth, unmistakably came Hopkins' response, "The money I hid…that I hid in that wood…I take its secret with me…and I will see you soon in hell."

Stearne straightened up again and looked down on the supine body of Hopkins. With a violent thrust his right hand gripped Hopkins' neck, causing him to exhale a strangled gasp of air that left his body with an unnatural squeal. Hopkins' desperate gurgles of breath caused spats of blood to scatter across the sleeve of Stearne's shirt, but still, in his terrible anger, he refused to release his grip.

"Where is my money, you villain! Where have you hidden my money!"

Hopkins' eyes blinked fully open before the colour within the irises seeped away. One final convulsion of air and blood vomited from Hopkins' mouth before his lifeless body sank back on the mattress, his head falling to one side, recumbent on the pillow. Stearne wiped Hopkins' sweat and blood from his sleeve on the bedsheet.

The secret of where the money was located had now been irretrievably lost. The brain that held its location had now begun its decline from living tissue to mere decaying matter.

Stearne, still angry with how Hopkins had once more outwitted him, strode over and pulled a wooden chair over to the bed. He then pulled back the bedsheets and roughly hauled the corpse into the chair. Hopkins body was slumped forward in a comically grim posture that caused Stearne to smile. Stearne opened the bedroom door, went to the head of the staircase and, after composing himself, called down, "Alice! Alice!"

The servant hurried to the foot of the stairs, "Yes, Mr Stearne?"

"Mr Hopkins is comfortable, so you must not vex yourself any more for the moment. You need rest. Go now, and return to your home and family. I will keep vigil with Mr Hopkins. You need to rest."

"But Mr Stearne..."

"Do as I say, Alice. There will soon come a day when we will require great things of you, and a fatigued Alice will be of little help to her master."

Alice crept away. Stearne went back into the room and watched from the bedroom window, his eyes following her as she walked out of the garden at the rear of the house towards her own cottage at the other end of Mistley village. Reassured that she was now gone, he went downstairs and walked out to an outbuilding at the side of Hopkins' house. Having been there so often in their early days, he knew exactly where to find what he was looking for. Sure enough, hanging on various nails along the wall, were various lengths of rope. After a few moments deliberation, he took down one rope, unfastened the loop and checked it for length. Satisfied, he returned to the house and went upstairs again to Hopkins bedroom.

The following morning, Alice was astonished to find that Matthew Hopkins' bed was empty, and its sheets pulled neatly up to the two pillows. Bewildered by what this might mean, she rushed downstairs and went from room to room calling, "Master Hopkins! Master Hopkins!" But he was nowhere to be found. Her heart raced with the excited notion that a great miracle had taken place, that her master had perhaps been cured and was sat this very moment looking out over the wide, brimless ocean or casually walking along the path to St Mary and St Michael's church to give thanks to God for his Lazarus-like recovery. But, to her increasing concern, he was neither inside the house, nor in any of the surrounding gardens or outbuildings.

Pulling her shawl over her head and shoulders, she decided to make for the village street to see if anyone else had seen him that morning. As she walked briskly along the High Street, she noticed a small crowd that had assembled around the deep pond that lay at the junction of two tracks. As she came nearer, she became aware that two men were hauling a rope and solemnly pulling something from the water. As the strange, and yet un-specified, object was pulled towards the shallow end of the pond, she slowly began to realise what it was that they were dragging towards the pond's edge. It was a man's dead body, roped to a wooden chair.

At first she recognised the chair. Then she recognised the body.

16

Manners Reveals All

My very dear Miss Smy

I trust that my letter finds you in good health.

Since our recent and - if I might express it thus - eventful meeting in Framlingham, I have pursued your request that I should seek out further information about Mr Houghton-Gale. In the time that I have been able to tear myself away from my onerous journalistic duties, I have endeavoured to do just that and I hope what follows meets with your approval.

According to my unimpeachable contacts, the Reverend Houghton-Gale commenced his current position within the parish of Layer de la Haye in 1912. Previously he was rector of Willersey in North Glouces-tershire. He took up this position in 1906 and, within months, had married a local woman. This would prove to be not the first time that he caused eyebrows to raise in the parish as his wife was a seamstress from - dare I say - not a very good home, and many thought that he had married beneath him.

But let me turn from matters domestic to matters controversial. The manner of his departure is most interesting. Apparently, a local farmworker, whilst ploughing a field adjacent to the parish church, turned over a store of Roman coins. The farmworker reported the find to the Reverend Houghton-Gale who immediately ordered that they be stored in his own vicarage for safekeeping, until local representatives could call upon the good Reverend to verify the treasure and take it back to the British Museum.

And now my tale twists in the most intriguing way. The following night, the vicarage was robbed whilst the Reverend Houghton-Gale was conducting Evensong in St Peter's Church. What seems uncommonly strange about this incident is that not only did the miscreants know exactly the location of the secreted coins, but that many other items of substantial value were in full display and yet left behind by the thieves.

I have also learned from a valued colleague who works for the Gloucestershire Echo, that the enquiry into the theft raised questions that Mr Houghton-Gale struggled to answer to the satisfaction of the local police. Although I do not have any means to corroborate what happened afterwards, it strikes me as most fortuitous that, two months later, Mr Houghton-Gale was suddenly offered a new position in a small parish many miles away in Essex.

Of course, you will know me as a person who must only believe in the good of those that populate these happy islands. But, if you may allow me a little hypothesis, purely for journalistic purposes of course, then it might be suggested that the two events - the discovery and ensuing theft of an invaluable hoard of Roman coins and the apparent expediting of Mr Houghton-Gale to the backwaters of a distant county - might be related. It is not within my power to pass judgement on such matters. My duty has been to faithfully relate these matters to you and leave such decisions in your fair hands.

I trust that the above information has been of some value to you and I seek no payment for these laborious queries which I have steadfastly conducted on your behalf. However, I wouldn't be in the least adverse to receiving a token of your appreciation in the form of another slice of your heavenly baking.

I remain, your most affectionate servant,

Nigel Manners Esq.

PS You will not have failed to observe, I'm sure, how your very presence so often causes me to feel most unnecessary. Upon reflection of what had passed between us in both of our recent intercourses, I would humbly beseech you to seriously and favourably consider that offer of marriage that I rather awkwardly communicated to you. My editor assures me that my prospects are exceedingly propitious, and it is that which causes me to feel bold enough to suggest that your current humble circumstances will be immediately elevated should you accept my proposal.

Winifred Smy looked at the *post scriptum* with her mouth agape in astonishment. She lay the letter down and, with a smile that honoured the brazen temerity of Nigel Manners Esquire, reached for her tea.

So Mr Houghton-Gale's boast was not an empty one. If the contents of Manners' letter were true, he really could engage in machinations 'most unbecoming to a man of the cloth'. But where did he fit into all of this?

On the table next to the letter was a copy of a newspaper that bore the headline: 'Police Murder Suspect Released - Essex Man Arrested and Charged'. The print below read:

The murder of Martha Ludbrook on the evening of June 25th has taken a dramatic twist. The original suspect, Mr Cecil Pallant, was immediately arrested and charged, but new clues have since come to light and Mr Pallant - a magician known to many as The Great Pazuzu - has been released and all charges dropped. Yesterday evening, officers of the East Suffolk Constabulary arrested another man for the crime, Dr Thurston Hessett, a bachelor from the town of Chelmsford in the county of Essex. Police have established that these new clues exonerated the previous suspect and place Dr Hessett firmly at the place and time of the murder.

Miss Smy could read no more. Perhaps one of the clues the police had recently discovered was the same as she had identified. That Dr Thurston Hessett's pretentious inclination for expressing himself in French had undoubtedly identified him as the murderer. Had he really, moments before the awful stabbing of Martha Ludbrook, pushed through the evening crowd with an apologetic 'Merci, merci'?

She was now convinced that she had started from the wrong foot, by instantly suspecting Mr Pallant just because he had so recently purchased the land within which the fake witchfinder had first appeared. Surely that was all a coincidence? Many people invest in land, but they can't be held accountable for the apparitions and behaviour that others may choose to demonstrate within them? And yet, and yet…

There was something that she felt distinctly uncomfortable about. She knew that, in some way that she so far failed to see, the hoard of coins and Adina's death were connected. The natural line that brought those two issues together was Mr Houghton-Gale; it was he that had revealed a criminal obsession with coins, if Mr Manners' letter was to be believed. And hadn't some vague connection to Martha Ludbrook clearly been demonstrated in his response to the news of her death? Yes, that seemed a line of enquiry that promised much. But what? Perhaps she was overthinking everything? Perhaps the police were right. It was Dr Hessett who had murdered Adina and there was simply nothing more to it.

"Mercy, mercy…" whispered Winfred Smy to herself.

With a violent jolt that sent her chair reeling backwards and on to its side, she sprang up and walked quickly about the room.

"Mercy, mercy," she again repeated as if it was some shadowy, exotic mantra.

She looked quickly in the mirror, tidied up some strands of hair that had become loose, slightly dipped her head to assure herself that she could reasonably present herself to the outside world before walking swiftly from her cottage, not even bothering to close the door behind her.

* * *

Agnes Stearne heard her husband wandering back and forth in his study. The constant creaking of the floorboards betrayed his agitation and, knowing those floorboards as intimately as Agnes did, she could tell exactly which side of the room he was at, at any one time. She placed down her prayer book and knocked on the door.

"John? John? May I come in?"

"Hmm? Oh, yes. Come in, Agnes."

She tried to enter the room in a breezy, unconcerned manner but was immediately struck by his appearance. "You've not washed. That's not like you."

"Haven't I? No, sorry, I haven't. Just dealing with a few things first."

"I was just thinking that you'd said that you wrote to Mother recently. What did she reply?"

"Oh, I've…I've not received anything yet. I'm sure we'll hear from her soon. You know your mother better than I, she's always very busy."

The nervous fidgeting of Agnes' fingers betrayed her own internal torment. She knew something was terribly wrong, but felt unable to press him on the matter. And there was something about his behaviour that only added to her discomfort. John Stearne seemed somehow defeated in his demeanour, but defeated by what, she couldn't tell.

"If something was wrong, you would tell me, wouldn't you? I think that you, of all men, would be the first to recall, 'Husbands, love your wives, and be not bitter against them'. Colossians, I think?"

"Colossians indeed. Chapter 3, verse 19. Or verse 18, I'm not sure which. And you should not become vexed. I am thoughtful, that's all. So be at peace, Agnes, for all is well." Stearne then turned and smiled at her. "Be gone, goodwife, and let me work. I am writing a book after all. And when a man writes a book, then he needs to search both memory and thought in an unhindered state. And that means being unhindered by his lovely wife even more."

Agnes smiled with a warm flush of embarrassment. "Ah yes, your book. Have you written anything yet?"

"Why yes, it is well under way and I am pleased with its progress. So go about your duties, Goodwife Stearne, and I will go about mine."

Agnes bowed her head a little and reluctantly backed out of the room. When she had left, John Stearne sat down and pulled a sheet of paper towards him. Once more taking his quill, he scrawled at the top of the page, *'A Confirmation and Investigation of Witch Craft'.*

He sat back in his chair and stared at the title, one hand idly rubbing the stubble of his cheek. He then dipped his quill into the inkwell and drew a line through what he had written. After a few more seconds of thought he wrote, *'A Confirmation and Discovery of Witch Craft'.*

The revised title pleased him and he immediately imagined what the front page of his book might look like. Was there a bible verse that might add more *gravitas* to his work? With a satisfied smile, he wrote beneath, "He that justifieth the wicked, and he that condemneth the just, even they both are abomination to the Lord."

In his mind, it was easy to line up all those, to one side or another, that he had encountered in his witch-finding career. Stearne himself headed the line of the just; Hopkins' insolent face - its pale skin marbled by the rank weeds of the pond from which he had been so humiliatingly extracted - marked the line of the wicked.

17

The Magic of
Misdirection

"Mr Pilbeam!"

Pilbeam, who had been smoothing the altar cloth, turned to see Miss Smy purposefully striding up the nave.

"Well, has a man no sanctuary these days? I take it from your enthusiastic approach that this is something that can't wait?"

Winifred Smy sat in the front pew and once again tried to give some shape to her hair. "It could wait but, as you well know, I'm not the waiting sort. All I need is some advice."

"Advice? A mere country rector like me? Why, I'd be exceeding my poor station in life. Tell me, is this a crisis of faith? If so, then I would rather enjoy my dinner first. It gives one the inner ballast to brave such tiresome conversations."

"No, not faith, but magic."

"Magic?"

"Yes, tell me about the principles of magic."

Pilbeam looked nonplussed by the turn in conversation. "Have you come to the right religion?"

"No. I've come to the right man. You have often delighted the Kenton schoolchildren with your conjuring and, although you are very modest about it, I am convinced that your modesty hides a considerable talent."

"Talent? Agreed. Considerable? If only. No, Miss Smy, I have a minor talent that will only impress the most junior of our parish. Nevertheless, I am gratified by your misplaced faith in my abilities."

"Please put that flippant manner to one side, Mr Pilbeam. You are a very intelligent man and I have the deepest respect for your person - in most things."

Pilbeam raised his eyebrows to acknowledge the limiting caveat so apparent in Smy's qualified praise.

"However," Smy continued. "I need to ask the principles you employ to create such wonderful deceptions. Last Christmas, the children loved your trick with those three cups and the ball. Every time that they guessed which cup the ball was under, you proved them wrong. How did you do it?"

Pilbeam walked into the nave and sat at the end of the opposite pew to Miss Smy. "How do I do it, Miss Smy? Simple. Misdirection."

"Misdirection?"

"The art of making those watching look at what you decide you want them to look at. Of course, because - through your encouragement - your audience has moved its collective gaze to something rather perfunctory, they will fail to notice the conjuror's sleight of hand or clever manipulation. Simple enough, but very baffling to those who are not aware of the art."

"So you move the focus of people's eyes so that they think they are looking at the most important part of the illusion, all so that they can't see what is really going on with the trick elsewhere?"

"In a nutshell, Miss Smy, yes. Here, do not look at my right hand!" Pilbeam held his right hand in the air with Smy's eyes instantly drawn to it. "There you are, misdirection. Any audience likes to believe that they are in control of where they choose to look but, in truth, it's the magician who chooses where the audience will look."

"I see. This is all very clever."

Pilbeam was now warming to his subject. "For example, with the cup and balls trick - which, I must point out, goes back at least to the times of the Romans - I often have not one ball but two. It's all very easy once you've distracted your audience enough, to slide a ball in or out from under a cup. Between ourselves, that trick was a useful source of income in my impoverished student days."

"Tell me, was it in those same impoverished student days that you first met Mr Houghton-Gale?"

"Why, Miss Smy, I do believe that you've slipped a different ball under the cup of our conversation. Yes, indeed, it was in Oxford that I initially encountered Mr Houghton-Gale. A very fine cricketer and a first-class mind to boot. As I remember it, he fell over me on 'the High'. I'd rather not explain why I was prostrate at the time, but we became firm friends and have remained in contact ever since."

Pilbeam reached for his pocket watch, thumbed the cover open and raised his eyebrows at what the clock face told him. "My stars, I'm running late. But tell me, dear Miss Smy. What is the real question? The one that you're really leading up to."

"Oh, I think you already know the question that I am leading up to."

Pilbeam laughed heartily. "You know I adore riddles. So, in the spirit of this delightful *divertissement*, I will give you the answer first and the question after. Agreed?"

Smy, enjoying Pilbeam's teasing manner, cheerily threw back, "Agreed."

"The answer is, no he is not. The question you wanted to ask was, is Mr Houghton-Gale a man of integrity? He is someone I have known for many years and, if pressed to capture the essence of the man, how would I describe him? Perhaps I might declare him as someone that values the friendship of others, whilst also able to ascertain in one sweep of their home the net worth of every piece of small and large *objet d'art* that graces each wall and cabinet."

"And does this want of integrity only apply to those items of art that can be bought and sold?"

Reverend Pilbeam stood and considered his response. "To Mr Houghton-Gale, I'm afraid everything can be bought and sold."

"That's a rather cynical attitude for a man of the cloth to have."

"A just weight and balance are the Lord's, Miss Smy, not ours. Whatever you may think of his fitness to carry out his religious calling, it is God that will judge his actions."

"Now you are annoying me, Reverend. Your reply seems to license the most iniquitous behaviour with the rather nebulous comfort that, despite their questionable actions here on earth, such men will eventually be brought to judgement on some distant day that we may eternally be waiting for."

The Reverend Pilbeam picked up the large keys from the pew at the rear of the church and flicked through them before finding the one he needed. "Yes, Miss Smy. To me it is most solemnly a comfort. To you, I fear, it is an empty promise. Perhaps that is why, since the sad passing of your Mother, we have not been graced by your presence at All Saints."

With a last reassurance that everything within the small church was in order, Pilbeam opened the large door that led into the South Porch, and beckoned Miss Smy to pass through it.

"Thank you for your time, Mr Pilbeam. I very much appreciated your truthfulness. But best of all, I enjoyed your explanation of your conjuring. I will watch with particular interest next time you entertain us with your magic show. Perhaps one day you might show me exactly how it is that you fool your audience so skilfully?"

Pilbeam looked up at the cloudless sky and closed his eyes with the sheer pleasure of the sun's heat. With eyelids still firmly closed, he replied, "I understand that there is a new organisation for magicians in London, which calls itself the 'Magic Circle'. I am not a member but must confess to being eager to adhere to its motto: *Indocilis private loqui*."

"My Latin has never been good but I take that to mean that you are not inclined to give away secrets?"

Pilbeam suddenly opened his eyes and smiled. "That is close enough a translation, Miss Smy. In an age of scientific revelation, we clergymen need all the mystery we can muster. Now, I must be heading home. Always delightful to talk with you. Oh, before I forget, the answer to your second question is, once again, no he is not."

"And my second question was?"

"Your second question was, is the Reverend Houghton-Gale a murderer?"

18

The Old Rugged Cross

"Your poor Miss Davison is getting a bashing from the press." Tranmer picked up a small bough and looked it over closely as if it was of some value. The day was very fine, with the heads of the faded cow parsley tipping slightly from side to side in the warm wind. "Her rushing headlong into the king's horse like that was utter madness."

"Yes, it's all rather depressing. 'A grotesque and meaningless kind of martyrdom', I think the *Pall Mall Gazette* called it. But it was not her intention to be a martyr. I'm certain about that."

"Certain? How can you be certain? Are you telling me she didn't want to die?"

"Look to the facts, Inspector."

"I thought we had agreed on Mr Tranmer?"

"This is a police matter to my mind and so I feel more comfortable addressing you in your professional capacity."

"Here we go again, I fear. So what are your 'facts'?"

"Let me lay them before you. My good friend - and a good friend of Emily's - Cicely Hale wrote to me and told me that they found on her person the return stub of a railway ticket back to London, and a ticket to a suffragette dance later that day. I would also add that her diary was full of appointments for the following week."

Tranmer nodded in agreement.

"So the question would naturally follow," continued Miss Smy. "Why would someone bent on suicide buy a return ticket? Why make sure that you bring a ticket to a later dance if you have no intention of attending? No, Inspector. It was a brave gesture that went horribly wrong. I will carry that conviction with me to the grave."

"Is that Leucock's Plantation, Miss Smy?" He indicated the copse ahead with his newly acquired stick.

"That's the one. The letter I read in the Chelmsford archive office, from Stearne to his mother-in-law, points out that the money was buried in 'a small plantation of trees owned by a Mr Leucock'. The plantation where the witchfinder was seen - Low Plantation - is the one we first went to."

"The one beside the railway track."

"The very same."

"I'm still puzzled by the same question, if you don't mind me repeating myself. Why would anyone want to draw attention to that plantation in such a way? I know that what you say about the spectre of witchcraft is still very strong in this area, but why feel the need to make the gesture? It makes absolutely no sense to me."

Tranmer offered his hand to Miss Smy so that it might steady her as she stepped over the small bridge that linked the field to the copse, but she looked at it with a withering and dismissive glance. "I am not quite helpless yet, Inspector."

Smy stepped into the plantation, steadied herself on the uneven ground and scrutinised what lay before her. The sun flickered and danced before them, its light tossed from leaf to leaf, dappling the Nightshade and what remained of the Dog's Mercury below.

"Back to your question about the witch finder's appearance. I'm beginning to formulate my own conclusions, but they are not ones that I wish to share at this moment. Nevertheless, if I am not exactly right in my hypothesis, I am convinced I am in the right area. And something in my very bones tells me that this is the right area."

To the Inspector's horror, a rustle of leaves announced the arrival of another party, who must have been standing on the other side of a mature holly.

"Good God, man! What are you doing?"

Smy turned and smiled. "Spadger! Delighted you were able to join us. You really must stop creeping around. You'll frighten the constabulary."

"The pleasure is mine, Miss Smy." With a swift movement, he removed his hat and bowed like the most ingratiating of courtiers.

"Inspector, meet Spadger Peck. You'll meet no finer man. An expert in so much of our Suffolk country life but probably even more proud of the fact that he has been banned from nearly all of the inns and taverns in this, and all the surrounding parishes."

Spadger now bowed before Tranmer. "Inspector. How yew a' diddl'n?"

"I was diddl'n just fine before you frightened me out of my wits."

Spadger looked at the Inspector with eyes narrowed, taking in the measure of the man. Having made his mind up about Tranmer, he turned to Miss Smy. "Oi met owd Tom yestdee, 'n' he say t' me 'Hev yew heard?'"

"And what were you supposed to have heard?"

"Tom said to me, 'e did, 'I reckon I'll ask that little owd mawther, Annie Cockrill to walk out with me'. Annie Cockrill, I sed. She's got a sting like a wapsy, I sed and…Hello, that's not right."

Spadger Peck was running the broad palm of his hand over an old tree stump that was no more than three feet high.

"What is it, Spadger?"

"Hold yew hard, Miss Smy, let me look now…Why, it's a cross. See here," Spadger traced the two lines of the cross with his finger. "No wonder they 'ad to fell this tree. Rum funny thing t' do, carvin' a cross loike that on it."

"Isn't that harmful to the tree?" Tranmer asked.

"Too right. Carve into any tree with a knife, why, you're openen it up to all sorts of 'arm. Killed this one."

"So that's why they had to cut it, Spadger? It was diseased?"

"Zactly. Shame though, thassa good ol' tree. Collar tells you that." Spadger pointed to the foot of the tree. "Won't survive a rove loike that, though."

"Why would someone do that, Spadger? These old plantations were farmed for wood, weren't they? Perhaps the owner was marking the tree he wanted cut down."

Spadger shook his head. "Look at that girth, too young for cutten. 'Sides, why not just take an axe to it?"

"Miss Smy, do you think it was made to mark a spot? If there was something buried here, you might need some way of locating where you'd left something."

Winifred Smy lay a hand on top of the stump and stared at the ground around it. "Inspector, that was my thought exactly. Whoever made this mark did so for a purpose and you and I are probably thinking the same thing, just what that purpose might have been."

"But all of this is academic, surely. Didn't you say that the money hidden in this copse had been stolen. Stearne's letter mentions that, if I remember right?"

"Ask yourself this, Inspector: if the money had been stolen, why does it continue to command the attention of three particular men? Pallant, whom I believe purposely bought these plantations purely so that he might discover Matthew Hopkins' hoard; Houghton-Gale, who also appears to take an uncommon interest both in coins and Stearne's archive files; Aand Doctor Thurston Hessett, who appears to have been prepared to murder Pallant's assistant, perhaps because he too was bent on recovering it."

"But if it's gone, surely it's a fool's errand?"

"No, Inspector, it is anything but a fool's errand. They know what I know. The money is still here. It always was here."

"How do you know? What makes you so convinced?"

"Because I still believe in magic. Don't you, Inspector?"

19

The Needling of Howard Houghton-Gale

"Miss Smy! This is a most unexpected pleasure. You really should have done me the courtesy of sending news of your arrival. I would have made sure that I was here to welcome you."

"I apologise for my unannounced visit. I had meant to send you a letter in advance but I regret that it rather slipped my mind."

"Slipped your mind? I have met you only once before today and, if I may say so, you do not strike me in the least as a 'slipped my mind' sort of person. Anyway, are you comfortable? Have you had some refreshment?"

Miss Smy reassured Mr Houghton-Gale that she had already had tea and was quite satisfied.

"I had a very pleasant talk with Mrs Houghton-Gale. Such an interesting woman who has known considerable hardship. I recall someone telling me before that, before she met you, she worked as a seamstress."

Houghton-Gale sat on the front edge of his desk and warily eyed Winifred Smy. "Indeed. A shocking profession to many. She worked long hours and…well, I'm sure I am just repeating what she has already told you."

"I must say that the quality of her stitching is perfection itself. Why, the very clothes your children wear are most becoming. It must be a comfort to have a wife who can make such economies in one's household. Tell me, does she make clothes for you?"

There was no answer from Houghton-Gale. He merely stood up and walked over to the large bay window. Eventually, he broke the silence. "My dear lady, I think you are playing games. I am pleased that you found your conversation with Selina instructive, but I am a busy man as I'm sure you will appreciate. Having arrived without notice, you must forgive me if I am un-able to accommodate you at such a busy time."

Winifred Smy stood and checked that she had her small bag and hat. "Such a coincidence that you had asked her to prepare some clothes for a masquerade that your old Oxford college was holding. And such a shame that it was all cancelled at the last minute. I'm sure that Mr Pilbeam and your professors would have been…"

"Leave!"

Miss Smy opened the door of the study only to quickly close it again. She walked back into the centre of the room and fixed Houghton-Gale with a steady eye.

"You do not fool me, Mr Houghton-Gale. You knew Martha Ludbrook. You knew her well. According to a friend of hers with whom I spoke only this morning, you struck up a rather close friendship. Oh, it was no more than that, but she was extremely taken with you."

"Are you about to accuse me of her murder? I would advise you to choose your next words with some care. Besides, they have now apprehended the real murderer as you'll know. Our dear demented Doctor Hessett. If you are not apprised of this development, then do help yourself to *The Colchester Gazette*. A copy is in the hall."

"You didn't murder her. And I am well aware that Doctor Hessett has now replaced Mr Pallant as the police's chief suspect. But that's not what I am referring to. I would be interested to know where you were on the 25th June?"

"Who the devil do you think you are? You inveigle yourself into my house, proceed to interrogate my wife after having the temerity to seek out the details of her private life, and then dare to put before me the half-formed musings of a mere woman! Now get out before I throw you out!"

"I am going. But I thought it rather pertinent that, as I was leaving on the last occasion, you quoted something rather appropriate for a numismatist. It was Shakespeare's *The Merchant of Venice*. I will not repeat the line in question, but I would draw your attention to two lines that quickly follow it: 'Gilded tombs do worms enfold. Had you been as wise as bold...'"

Miss Smy unhurriedly turned and left the study with a racing heart, but was determined to demonstrate to Houghton-Gale that she would leave the house on her own terms. She wished she had had the time to deliver the *coup de grâce* to

Houghton-Gale before she had quit the vicar's study: 'Fare you well. Your suit is cold.'

Still shaken by the anxious intensity of her meeting, she pushed her bicycle out from the vicarage garden, mounted it and set off to ride the five miles back to Colchester Station. The sun, which had now climbed to its full height, threw down an oppressive heat and only the softness of the air as it swept across her face brought some relief as she rode along the lanes.

When she had reached Colchester, she cycled down the High Street and on to the grounds that surrounded the castle. Laying down her bicycle, she looked up at the forbidding walls and immediately brought to mind Elizabeth Albrey. Dragged from her Kenton cottage and, after a confession had been cruelly extracted from her, imprisoned in this coffin fortress. Here it was, as Mr Houghton-Gale had informed her during Miss Smy's previous visit, that Elizabeth Albrey had perished.

She found a spot on the grass where she could sit, and watched the sheep slowly roaming across the grounds, ignorant of the innumerable tragedies that these few acres had witnessed. Winifred Smy, a woman who had found herself caught in a struggle for freedom, was now thinking of another woman whose limited freedoms were snatched away over two centuries ago.

And what about Martha Ludbrook? Was she yet another woman whose life stood in a tragic parallel to Elizabeth Albrey's? Hadn't her life too been snuffed out by the whim of a man? Whatever the part Martha Ludbrook had played in the mysterious events that Winifred Smy was now confidently teasing apart, she deserved an infinitely better fate than the one that had befallen her.

Smy felt a loneliness creep into her heart. Where now was the irritating and intrusive patter of Nigel Manners, the steadfast entreaties of Hebert Tranmer, or the impish observations of the Reverend Pilbeam? She would have welcomed the company of any of them, but knew they were all engaged elsewhere and would have been surprised to learn that she was carrying such frailties and moments of doubt within her. Mr Houghton-Gale had unnerved her. His response to her observations had told her that, at last, she was within touching distance of why Martha Ludbrook had been murdered.

She picked up her bicycle and prepared to ride the remaining mile or so back to the station. As she rode across the River Colne and into Kings Meadow, she decided upon a change of plan. She would not take the train back to Haughley and then on to Kenton, but return via Framlingham, changing at Ipswich station.

If Inspector Tranmer was indeed unaware of the agitation of Miss Smy's mind, then she would soon set him right.

*　　*　　*

Try as she might, Agnes Stearne could find no love in her heart for her husband. It had been 13 years since the death of Matthew Hopkins and that death had seemed to mark a slow, relentless dwindling of their fortunes. They had been blessed - or was it burdened - with even more children who had survived.

Even the sums that had resulted from the sale of John Stearne's remaining properties in Manningtree had soon disappeared.

Stearne had, in his increasing desperation, turned to legal action in increasingly hostile exchanges with his neighbours concerning matters connected to his properties. Yet even when judgement fell on his side, the recompense was poor. And now he lay in their bed, breathing unsteadily and tortured by the pain of the cancer that was slowly eating him from the inside out. In rare moments of consciousness, he emerged from the confusion of his addled mind to rail against past wrongs.

"The hole! Look to the hole, I tell you! The money is gone. He's taken the money. Edward, he's taken the money. I had to tell her. She didn't believe me. Oh, please God, I had to tell her..."

Agnes calmly continued reading, her prayer book open on her lap. No, all love had gone. She thought of her father, the doubts long ago he had shared when she had first introduced Stearne to her parents. Stearne had land and prospects, but there was a flaw in his being that she had failed to notice. What she thought of as an innate self-assuredness was eventually revealed to be an intolerance for anyone's opinion but his own. His strength was an ignorance of his failings, and his failings were many.

Perhaps there had been a notion of love at the beginning? She vaguely recalled a genuine bond between them, the faith that they both shared in a different future. But, since his return from the travels of his witch finding days, they had sunk slowly into a respectable poverty. And with the fall in their income, their standing in the community had declined at a similar rate.

Agnes Stearne became alarmed with the awful realisation that she thought she had been praying so that her husband might live. In truth, as she now recognised, each prayer was a call to God that he would die.

Unable to bear the irritating rasps and gulps for air that irregularly emanated from Stearne's throat, she put down her prayer book and went downstairs. Now she could enter and wander around his study at will. On the bookshelf adjacent to the fireplace, next to Stearne's heavily annotated bible, she caught sight of a pamphlet. Unlike the bible, it was in an almost pristine state. She took the pamphlet down and realised that it was the original author's copy of Stearne's apologia, *'A Confirmation and Discovery of Witch Craft'*. She leafed through page after page of arguments and biblical references all serving to vindicate the actions of the witchfinders all those years ago. She closed the pamphlet between the palms of her small hands and went through into the main room of the house where Bessie had lit a good fire, the logs crackling and spitting in the grate.

Agnes Stearne was not yet to know that, at the very moment that she tossed the reviled pamphlet into the flames, her husband was sputtering his final breath.

20

One's Elusive Mr Lacey

The heavy door was opened and Miss Smy found herself in a small room, unfurnished save for a single chair positioned directly in front of a metal grille that separated the prisoner from their visitor. She sat down and waited. After a few minutes a door was opened on the prisoner's side and the diminished figure of Thurston Hessett entered, followed by a guard. The guard stood against a wall with his arms folded behind.

"Good morning, Doctor Hessett. I hope you do not mind my asking to see you?"

Hessett sat on the chair, removed his cap and stared incongruously through his side of the grille at Miss Smy. "One is confused. Very confused. When they told me that I had a visitor and that visitor was you, one could not for the life of one think why you should want to see me. Miss Smy, why are you here? Oh, please understand, the chance to talk with someone, anyone, is most welcome. As you can see, one's circumstances are somewhat reduced since we were last together."

Smy felt a horror run through her as she saw the rough prison clothes Hessett was wearing. As Hessett was speaking to her, she struggled to clear her mind of the degrading experiences she had once suffered at the hands of the wardresses of Holloway.

"Doctor Hessett, I met with Inspector Tranmer of the East Suffolk Constabulary yesterday afternoon and asked if I could visit you today. I know something of the events that have been in motion surrounding the reasons why you were arrested. I want to help you, I am utterly convinced I can help you - but to do so, I need to ask you some questions that you may find intrusive."

"One has already been stripped of all dignity. There is no private or personal space left to one that you can intrude upon, I assure you."

"I know that you have been accused of the murder of Martha Ludbrook. I also know that you will have been asked a great many questions. Have you no alibi for the night in question? Is there nobody who can vouch for you? Someone who saw you perhaps?"

"One can only tell you what one has already told the police. On the very morning I went to Ipswich, I received a letter - delivered by one of his servants - from a Mr Lacey, asking if I would be willing to give my opinion as to the authenticity of a map he had discovered whilst clearing his recently deceased father's loft. You may not know it, but one has something of a reputation for historical maps and so, naturally, I was excited about the discovery. If I accepted, then Mr Lacey promised to send the funds to cover my return passage from Chelmsford to Ipswich station."

"What was the address of Mr Lacey?"

"The address of the letter was 5, Museum Street. But Mr Lacey asked one to meet him at 7.00 pm in Westgate, on the corner of Providence Street, which was the apparent address of his late father's house."

"And Mr Lacey never showed up?"

"He certainly didn't. One waited for over half an hour and then thought that something might have happened to him."

"And then you returned home?"

"Not quite. It occurred to one that he might still be at home and, I admit to being so excited about the prospect of inspecting the map, I thought it worthwhile visiting his house to see if he was there and had perhaps forgotten."

Smy leaned forward in her chair, "And what did you find?"

"An empty house. The address was respectable enough, but the place was entirely vacant. One looked through the windows and there were some furnishings, curtains and carpets and things, but it was clear that the property was vacant."

"And then?"

"And then one went home. One must admit to being bemused by the whole evening, but little did one know what it was all going to lead to. I must admit one could never have guessed in one's wildest imaginings that one's next visit to Ipswich would be as a resident of its gaol."

Miss Smy smiled but could not fail to be moved by his appearance. That slightly arrogant demeanour had vanished and not once had he spoken to her in French. With the guard in such close attention, Hessett probably knew that it would be seen as some secret code between the two of them and only add to the seriousness of his situation.

"I hesitate to repeat my question, Doctor Hessett, but is there no one who can stand for you on the night Martha was murdered? Did you talk to anyone perhaps, whilst you were waiting for the fictitious Mr Lacey?"

Hessett hung his head and stared at where his folded hands rested in his lap. "One spoke to no one. Not one soul from the moment one arrived in Ipswich until one boarded one's train back to Chelmsford. But why would they think I murdered this poor woman? I didn't even know her."

"What evidence have they obtained other than the witnesses' testimony that the killer was speaking French?"

"Oh, that's the cleverest move of all. You see, the letter I sent to Mr Lacey provided a perfect template of one's writing. In the letter I said things like, 'I am very much looking forward to meeting you and so forth. But they have forged my hand! The letter is even addressed to Adina and contains words I never wrote. It's even written on paper that matches one's own stationery."

"Which would be easy enough to steal when you were out obtaining any files that had been requested. I saw the very same stationery myself, on your side desk."

"The most upsetting thing of all is that the police then told me that Miss Ludbrook was stabbed with a letter opener. And it was one's letter opener they discovered at the crime scene, with one's fingerprints all over it! For pity's sake, who would want to do this to me? I have never done anyone any harm. One thinks one has no enemies. Perhaps I'm incorrigibly naïve. Maybe one does have people who dislike one. But to do this to me. Why?"

With a weak smile, Winifred Smy tried to reassure him, but knew there was nothing that she could say that would make him feel better.

"Doctor Hessett, when I first came to your premises, you told me that there had been three people who had asked for the same file I requested. Do you remember that conversation?"

"Of course. The Stearne file. One remembers the gentlemen quite distinctly."

"I can tell you that they were the Reverend Houghton-Gale, a vicar from Layer de la Haye; Nigel Manners, a journalist from Framlingham; and Cecil Pallant, a well-known magician. I take it that you are aware that Martha Ludbrook was Mr Pallant's stage assistant?"

She could see that Thurston Hessett was beginning to grow tired. "Yes, Miss Smy, that fact has been shared with one. But one really doesn't see where you are going with this."

"Please be patient with me. I am trying to help you as best I can. Let me make it plain: I do not believe that you murdered Martha Ludbrook."

At this, tears dropped from Hessett's face onto his small crossed hands. His shoulders lurched as he wept, "Oh, thank God someone believes one, because one is at one's wits end. I couldn't kill another person. Why would they think I could?"

"Listen to me, Dr Hessett. First, compose yourself because I want to ask you something, and I need your mind to be clear when you answer."

Hessett drew a deep breath, sniffled and then dabbed his nose with his sleeve. "I'm sorry, I really am. It's all been rather too much for one. This foul place. These awful clothes. One's cell is utterly appalling."

"I know."

"How could you know? You've never been through what I've been through."

"I will tell you this and no more: I have been through worse than you. Believe me most sincerely, sir, I know the misery that you endure."

Hessett looked up at Miss Smy, but still could not comprehend the full import of what she was telling him.

"Excuse me, Dr Hessett, but there's a small feather in your hair."

Hessett reached up and brushed the top of his head. "Probably some poor bird sharing the prison yard with one. They let one walk around it for a short time."

"It's gone now. So, can I ask you my question?"

"Of course. Ask as many questions as you like."

"When I was in your office, you'll remember that I asked first for John Stearne's files. And then, when I was about to leave, I asked for another file, which you then brought me."

"Yes, that's right."

"Did the gentlemen I referred to earlier ask for the same file?"

Hessett thought for a moment. "Why, yes, two of them did."

"Who was the person that didn't ask for that file?"

"The man you said was from Framlingham. The skinny, awkward chap."

Miss Smy sat back in her chair and closed her eyes. "Doctor Thurston Hessett, I truly believe the pieces of this tragic mystery are finally falling into place."

21

And His Holy Arm hath gotten Him the Victory

That morning there had been heavy showers and, looking from her window, Miss Smy decided that the sky was now sufficiently clear for her to walk to Debenham. When she reached 'The Causey', the long tree-lined path that linked the village of Kenton to Kenton Hall, she found herself gaining on the Reverend Pilbeam, who was ambling slowly ahead of her.

"I think we are in for another warm day now the rain has cleared, Mr Pilbeam?"

"Why, it's Miss Smy! Forgive my not noticing you, but the ground in July is truly abundant with so much of nature's most beautiful things."

When Pilbeam walked along any stretch of grass or disappeared into some bosky glade, his eyes immediately looked downwards, ready to espy any shy flower or retiring shrub that lay hidden beneath.

"The bluebells have gone but their friends remain. I love the Greater Stitchwort. *Stellaria holostea*, Miss Smy. And what I love most about it is its deceptiveness."

"You are referring to the petals, I take it?"

"Why, yes. You're absolutely right. The unobservant would count ten petals. But the observant, as you certainly are, know that each of the five petals is deeply notched. Nature has a way of upsetting our preconceptions, I often think."

"On the subject of upsetting one's preconceptions, I must warn you that I may have rather upset your friend, Mr Houghton-Gale."

"Nothing to do with me. I only introduced you. Your behaviour in each other's company must be your own affair. Oh, now there is a late bluebell. How entrancing."

"One can't help noticing that he has little of the Christian about him. Perhaps I have not seen him at his best?"

Pilbeam laughed at her observation. "Well, there are many unchristian souls within the clergy; I've met one or two myself."

"Surely that's an oxymoron? An unchristian vicar?"

"Not at all! In the same way that the devil of a headache can cure one of the desire for alcohol, constant exposure to the religious life can drain every shred of belief a man might have. To some it's a calling; to others, it's merely their occupation."

They walked in silence together for some minutes before Miss Smy said, "I've been thinking deeply about the churchwarden's letter. Can I share my thoughts with you?"

"Share away, Miss Smy. I've had one or two musings about that very missive myself."

"I warn you, this will only be a hypothesis, so I would warmly welcome your opinion."

"Sharing my opinion is second only to sharing my cricket anecdotes, and the veracity of both is equally dubious."

"I am convinced that the Reverend Geffrey was murdered. What unsettled me continually was the description of his arm. Even our faithful churchwarden, Mr Mouser, who had seen considerable bloodshed in battle, couldn't account for it. So I contacted a medical friend I knew from my London days with my suspicions."

"And did he confirm your suspicions?"

"Not all eminent people in the medical profession are men, Mr Pilbeam."

"Oh, he was a she?"

"Her name is Mrs Garrett Anderson."

Pilbeam stopped and held his hand to his forehead whilst he thought. "Garrett Anderson...Garrett...The mayor of Aldeburgh! Of course! You knew her in London? Well, what a rich history you have. You know, Miss Smy, you never fail to astonish me."

"My suspicion, if I may return to the subject in hand, was that Mr Geffrey's arm was in such a position due to *rigor mortis*. Wherever he had died, it had not been in the place that he was found, otherwise his body and limbs would have been completely on the ground. I would propose that he had been killed elsewhere and his body kept in a confined area such that his limbs reflected that confinement when the *rigor mortis* set in."

"So, you are saying that the unfortunate vicar was slain (how I shudder when I think of such an abominable thing) in a place where there was limited movement, and then deposited some-time later at the foot of the tower?"

"Quite so, with the theatrical arrangement of a stone placed nearby, and his skull appropriately crushed, so as to suggest quite another reason for his death."

Miss Smy turned to gauge Mr Pilbeam's reaction but found herself looking at an empty space. Turning she could see him some twenty metres back or so peering at what appeared to be a small apple. She smiled as she looked at his familiar gaze when entranced by the natural world: his head cocked slightly back and his mouth opened in keen concentration.

"Were you listening?" she enquired.

"Of course! The vicar was killed elsewhere and left at the foot of the tower with matters arranged so that no one would suspect murder. But look at this, *Biorhiza pallida*. The Oak Apple Gall Wasp. Quite wonderful. This little apple contains a number of chambers, each housing a larva that will eat its way out. Quite stupendous."

"And my hypothesis?"

"Quite sound. Quite sound, indeed." Pilbeam smiled at Winifred Smy, removed his glasses and rubbed them on his sleeve. "That's better," he observed as he held the lenses up to-wards the sky.

"Thank you for your attention," said Miss Smy sarcastically. But her dry wit was lost on the good Reverend, who merely smiled and walked on.

"So now you have a murder, but no murderer. Does your hypothesis extend to that?"

Miss Smy quickened her pace to catch up with him. "Henry Mouser draws particular attention to Hopkins' and Stearne's assistant, Edward Parsley. Perhaps Geffrey witnessed something he shouldn't have. Who knows? Such things are lost…"

"I hope you are not going to say 'in the mists of time', Miss Smy. Some clichés can considerably weaken one's *vim vitae.*"

"But the strangest thing is that Edward Parsley disappears from life, quite suddenly. He was a Manningtree man, so I asked my good friend Mrs Horlock (she was a Suffolk girl originally) to investigate. Her letter told me that the church at Manningtree dutifully records his baptism and marriage, but that there is no mention of him after that."

"Then he died elsewhere. That's not unusual. Your next task is to investigate every parish register of the land to determine where he expired. That's something to preoccupy you for the next few months, eh, Miss Smy?"

Pilbeam became quickly aware that all was not right and he turned to see that Miss Smy was walking angrily back down the Causey towards her home.

"You are too brittle a creature sometimes, Miss Smy," he said aloud to himself. "Too brittle indeed." But how deeply he admired her. She had principles. She held dear to a cherished set of beliefs about what was decent and true. But she was sensitive, very sensitive, too sensitive. An unkind word, an ill-thought through gesture would inflame her anger. Pilbeam watched her slowly diminishing figure with a rueful smile.

"All men should marry a Miss Smy," he pondered. "The trouble is that Miss Smys do not want to be married to men."

22

The Sinister Hand

"Ah, Mr Houghton-Gale. You're late. Your telegram told me to meet you here at three o' clock, precisely. I do very much detest lateness."

"My telegram? I didn't send any telegram. It was your message that brought me here. I apologise for being late, but the train was late leaving Haughley. I take it that you are Mr Pallant?"

Pallant's face became serious, "Have you brought the telegram with you?"

"No, I thought it safer to throw it away. But it just said to meet at Leucock Plantation, 3pm today, do not reply. Pallant."

"Exactly what my message said, with your name as the sender. This is very disconcerting. Very disconcerting indeed."

Pallant shot a panicked look about him. The copse appeared deserted, but he began to feel as if a trap had been set. Houghton-Gale remained much more composed and started to pick off strands and seeds of goosegrass that had attached themselves to his trousers and boots.

"I was very sorry to hear about the murder of your Adina. That must have been an awful shock for you. I read that you had been released by the police. Was Adina with you for very long?"

"You should know the answer to that, Mr Houghton-Gale."

Houghton-Gale simply raised his eyebrows before laconically replying, "Why so?"

But Pallant now refused to be drawn in and looked slowly around once more.

Houghton-Gale grew impatient. "Somebody is playing games with you and I, I fear, and I have a sneaking suspicion who that person might be."

"Are you going to tell me?"

"Halloo! What a coincidence!" Winifred Smy waved from the field path and immediately picked her way carefully into the plantation.

"Oh, I hope I don't dirty this dress. It's clean on only this morning."

Houghton-Gale and Pallant darted sharp glances at each other as Miss Smy approached.

"Mr Pallant, are you looking over your estate? It's beautifully shady here, don't you agree? A stiflingly hot day. I was halfway down Church Lane and thought whether I should go back for my parasol, but it was too tedious a thing to do and here I am, soldiering on. Mr Houghton-Gale! I never knew that you and Mr Pallant were acquainted. How extraordinary!"

"Did you send those telegrams, Miss Smy? I would put good money on it being your work."

"Me? Telegrams? Why would I send you telegrams?"

Pallant reached into his pocket and handed her his copy. "This arrived today. Look for yourself."

Winifred Smy scanned the piece of paper. "I can assure you it wasn't me that sent your telegrams. You have my word on that."

"Then who the blast did?"

"Mr Houghton-Gale, your language! It's most unbecoming for a man of the cloth. But then you did once tell me that you have often been unbecoming for a man of the cloth. I am aware that Mr Pilbeam..."

"I have had enough of this tomfoolery! If it wasn't you then who did arrange for me and Pallant to meet here? And if it's their idea of a joke, then I would not hesitate to beat them most severely for it."

"Have patience, man," snapped Pallant. "Miss Smy, what are you doing here? Don't tell me that you were just passing. That would be taking incredulity too far."

Winifred Smy allowed a half-smile to rest momentarily on her lips, before her face grew suddenly serious. "Why did you kill Martha Ludbrook, Mr Pallant?"

"What? What the devil are you saying, you foolish woman? How dare you! The man that killed Martha is at this moment in Ipswich Gaol, as you well know. And if you don't, then pray consult a newspaper."

"The man that killed Martha Ludbrook is standing right in front of me now, Mr Pallant. You know it and I know it. It was you that stabbed her that fateful evening. You have just confirmed that very fact when you handed me this telegram."

"Are you mad? You are mad! What the blazes are you wittering on about? Hessett killed Martha Ludbrook. The police have their man and you have lost your wits, Miss Smy."

"The trouble is that you are a great man of the theatre. But the dividing line between your public theatrical life has been allowed to blur with the personal theatrical life. You watch how the audience is utterly stupefied by your act. They have no answer as to how you achieve your dazzling feats of magic - or should I correct myself and say 'illusion'?"

"I think I should leave. This is nothing to do with me."

"Oh, do stay Mr Houghton-Gale. We both know that you played your own part in it as well."

"I think you're mistaken, dear lady!"

"I am not your 'dear lady' and you would do well to remember that fact. I would like to come to your part in this tawdry and tragic matter in a moment."

Smy turned back to Pallant and asked, "May I continue? I intend to anyway."

"Then why ask?" sneered Pallant.

"It was the wonderful Reverend Pilbeam who cleared away so much of my confusion. He is but an amateur illusionist, although a very good one, and he informed me of the magician's principle of 'misdirection'. You make people look where you want them to look. And there was no finer demonstration of that trickery than the way that you killed Martha. I admit it was utterly ingenious. Arrange it so that you initially look like the murderer but leave small clues that will draw attention to where you wanted them to really look: at poor Doctor Thurston Hessett."

"This is just fantasy, Miss Smy. I take my hat off to you and your wonderful imagination."

"Ah yes, the hat. The homburg hat and the cape with the red lining, both skilfully deposited *en route* to Ipswich train station. Hidden, but not too well hidden or someone wouldn't have been able to find them. More misdirection, Mr Pallant. Why, you even delivered the letter summoning Doctor Hessett to Ipswich that evening yourself. Oh, I grant I can't be certain of that, but the door keeper remembered that you walked straight into the building and found the room yourself. Unless that servant was a person who had called previously at the archivist's office, how would they be able to go straight to the room without at least asking directions?"

"That doesn't mean it was me!"

"And that doesn't mean it was not you. But it was the letter opener that was the final clue."

"Don't waste your breath telling me that it was not Doctor Hessett's letter knife! The police have told me that it definitely belonged to him!"

"Well, I can tell you categorically that it was Doctor Thurston Hessett's knife. And that was your next mistake. Having delivered a letter to him, you would expect him to immediately reach for his letter knife to open it. But, hey presto - as I think an amateur might announce it - the knife had gone! Doctor Hessett was dumbfounded. He swore to me when I visited him in prison that it had been on his desk moments before because he had already opened the first post with it. No, only an illusionist could have spirited that letter opener away with such aplomb."

"He'd probably lost it. We all lose things from our desks."

"Not if it was to be the murder weapon, Mr Pallant."

"Your fantasy has reached the giddiest heights, Miss Smy, but I am grown quite nauseous with it all. I am leaving immediately, which I suggest you do as well, otherwise I would be obliged to treat your continued presence as trespass."

"Can I return this before I am made to go?" Pallant took the telegram back from Miss Smy.

"Yes, once again, you confirm it was you who stabbed Miss Ludbrook."

"What are you talking about? It's a telegram! How can a telegram have any meaning in all this!"

"I understand a witness made the following statement, and I quote exactly here, 'The assailant grabbed her shoulder and the knife entered just below her right shoulder blade.'"

"I am none the wiser."

"You may be none the wiser, Mr Pallant, but you are about to be all the better informed. The murderer approached Martha from behind and stabbed her. If it was to be below the right shoulder blade, which was how it would be described from a medical person standing in front of her, then the assailant must have stabbed her in the left-hand-side of her back whilst their right hand would have held her opposite shoulder."

"How can you be so sure?"

"Because the witnesses corroborated the way Martha was murdered. So, it couldn't possibly have been Doctor Thurston Hessett, who - when I saw him - unwittingly revealed that he was right-handed when I pretended that there was a small bird's feather in his hair. He instinctively used his right hand to brush it away. Whereas, when you handed me the telegram and then took it back, you used your left hand on both occasions."

"Is this all true, Pallant? What Miss Smy is saying? Is it true, man?"

"Nothing she is telling you is true."

"Oh, can I just ask, *quand avez-vous appris à parler français, Monsieur Pallant?*"

"What are you saying? Speak English, woman!"

"No, I thought not. If it truly had been Thurston Hessett who had murdered Martha that night, his superb pronunciation would never have mangled the simple French word for 'thank you': 'merci'. Again such amateurism, Mr Pallant. I would respectfully suggest a decent French teacher if mimicking other languages is to become an extension of your current theatrical offering."

Pallant's simmering temper was now beginning to come to the boil, and Smy saw her chance to strike. "Quite simply, you framed Doctor Hessett so that the police would think the whole event a clumsy attempt by him to make it look like you. But such an amateur illusion, Mr Pallant. Really, as a professional of some years standing, I would have thought you capable of so much better."

A now furiously angry Cecil Pallant stepped back and jerked out a small pistol from inside his jacket. "Get over there, both of you! Get over there!"

"What are you doing, Pallant?" cried a visibly shaken Houghton-Gale.

"I know what I'm doing! And I always knew what you were doing. You and Adina were thick as thieves, weren't you? You thought I didn't know what you were up to, but you under-estimated me, Houghton-Gale."

"I didn't know the woman. Why are you dragging me into all of this?"

"Because you dragged yourself into all of this. You knew about the coins. You were the one that started miraculously appearing to passers-by on the train, dressed - of all things - as a witchfinder. You and Martha wanted me out of the way. So your plan was to spook everyone. The villagers, me, so that no one would want to come near this place or any place round here. You deliberately left a rope in the wood, a rope that she had stolen, and that would then lead people back to me. And then busybody Miss Smy here put your two and two together. Big illusion in the wood and a new owner who is an illusionist. You wanted to make it so that people would start asking questions. As our dear Miss Smy did. How could I go looking after those coins with all that publicity in the area?"

"You're a fool if you think that, Pallant. It wasn't me."

"Oh, it was you, all right. Martha told me as much when I had her under hypnosis."

"Hypnosis?" exclaimed Winifred Smy.

"Of course. I'm not some magician one-trick pony. And when you came snooping around in the cafe that day, I knew not to mention it. Have you ever asked yourself who the man was with Martha on the night she died, the man that was walking a few yards ahead? Why, you're about to die alongside him."

"Killing us would be a mistake, Mr Pallant," urged Smy. "I'm not the only one that knows what I have just shared with you."

"No, but the evidence is so circumstantial, I will take my chances with the half-wits that are the Suffolk Constabulary and arrange today's events so that it will look like you were both involved in the awful mess. Then I will have all the time in the world to find those coins."

"Coins like this one, Mr Pallant?" Smy held a dull, mud-tarnished coin aloft. Pallant and Houghton-Gale's eyes widened in astonishment. Then a metallic double-click sounded behind Pallant.

"Drop that gun now, or I'll give yew both these 'ere barrels, Mr Pallant. Did yew really think Miss Smy 'ould come in 'ere by 'ersel? Why you really must think that mawther wuz sorft in the hid."

23

In Rose Lemonade
There is Truth

By the time Spadger Peck had regaled most of the pub-going population of the parish of Debenham, the story of his involvement in the arrest of Cecil Pallant had assumed almost mythical proportions. In fact, with each boozy retelling, his place at the margin of the event had gradually given way to a version where he was the main proponent, and poor Miss Smy's role firmly relegated to that of a bit-part player.

Of course, the news of the events that had taken place in Leucock Plantation had been exclusively presented to the Suffolk reader by none other than Mr Nigel Manners of the *Framlingham Weekly News*; it was Miss Smy's way of thanking him for the important research that he had undertaken on her behalf.

Winifred Smy herself had just finished writing a letter to Nigel Manners, and she held it up - executed in her neat

copperplate handwriting - to satisfy herself that it was clear in
its message.

Dear Mr Manners

*I apologise for not having been able to find the time to respond to
your recent reminder of your original proposal of marriage.*

*I am quite aware that you have great talents and am unsurprised
that these are being acknowledged by those to whom you report. I also
appreciate that your pecuniary prospects are extremely favourable; it
is well documented that where poverty is present, relationships can
experience enormous strain.*

*Yet I feel I must decline your gracious offer. It is rather old-
fashioned of me but these pecuniary elements - although they have
their place - are nothing if there is no love present. You do not love
me and I do not love you. I fear that you see relationships as mere
business arrangements; I see relationships as something much deeper
and fulfilling.*

*Would you grant me leave to offer some advice? When you do
find the woman of your dreams and wish to communicate your desire
that you both wed, do not consign your proposal to a post scriptum in
a letter. I think you will find my suggestion will ensure that future
offers of marriage meet with infinitely more success.*

With every good wish

Winifred Smy

She folded the letter neatly and placed it in an envelope
already addressed to Manners' office. After picking up a large

cotton handbag which appeared to contain a heavy book, she then walked the short distance to the vicarage where she was met by Hannah, the Reverend Pilbeam's servant, who led her through the house into the capacious, long garden at the rear of the building. The late afternoon sun began to stretch long shadows across the neatly clipped lawn that fell before the oaks and ash. Hidden in a nearby hawthorn, the pitch of some young blackbird chicks' cheeps grew as their parent hovered over the nest with a writhing meal.

"My dear Miss Smy, it's lovely that you are able to join us." Agatha Pilbeam, the Vicar's dutiful and much put-upon wife, had features which, in themselves were plain when seen in isolation, but combined in the most attractive way when irradiated by her smile.

Chairs had been arranged around a large table on which sat a variety of sandwiches, cold meats and delicate cakes, accompanied by tall glasses and a large jug of rose lemonade. In two of the chairs - although both men now rose to greet her - had been sitting Herbert Tranmer and Mr Pilbeam. Tranmer and Smy looked at each other with surprise. Neither had been expecting the other to be there and it occurred to her that the vicar and his wife may well have colluded to bring the two together again.

"That's a very lovely dress you have Mrs Pilbeam. Is it new?"

"It is kind of you to notice."

"A London fashion, surely?"

"Well, yes. That's very astute of you. I recently received a very small bequest and so thought I would add something to my somewhat tired wardrobe."

Chairs were pulled back by the men and both Agatha Pilbeam and Winifred Smy seated themselves.

Pilbeam clapped his hands with considerable enthusiasm. "Now I will pour you all a glass of this delicious lemonade but you, dear Miss Smy, must explain everything. I've picked a shred of a story here and a scrap of detail there but can't quite piece everything together. I am relying on you to do this for me."

"Yes," added his wife. "You cannot leave our garden until we are completely satisfied that we have gleaned everything you know. Once again you are quite the talk of the village."

Winifred Smy looked towards Inspector Tranmer, "Surely you can convince these good people that, compared to your work, what I have done is very small beer?"

Tranmer shook his head, "I was talking with Nigel Manners and he knows some things and I know some things but, as Mr Pilbeam said, you are the guardian of the entire body of facts, so I am all ears as well, I'm afraid."

Miss Smy smiled ruefully and sat up in her chair. "Then we must go a long way back if you want to know everything. Mr Pilbeam, you'll remember the letter that you first showed me?"

"Henry Mouser's letter? The churchwarden chappie?"

"That's the one. That was what first piqued my interest. But it actually all started with Gladys, Gladys Cupper. She arrived at my house with a most extraordinary tale, that she had seen from the window of her train a witchfinder in Low Plantation, with a woman hanging from a tree close by him. At first I thought it was someone play-acting, but then you, Mr Pilbeam, drew my attention to that curious letter written by Kenton's church-warden in 1647."

"Ah yes, the one about the visit of two witchfinders who accused some poor Elizabeth Albrey of dealings with the devil? Quite extraordinary."

"Poor Elizabeth Albrey," said Agatha Pilbeam. "I read the letter myself. And he also recalled the accidental death of Mr Geffrey, the vicar at the time."

Miss Smy turned to Agatha Pilbeam. "With Mr Geffrey, I am convinced that was no accident. The facts pointed otherwise. I can't say for certain of course, but my guess is that the Reverend Geffrey was murdered elsewhere and his body deposited at the foot of the tower with a large stone placed nearby to make it look like an accident. But Mouser had his doubts and so did I. We will never know why the vicar was killed, perhaps the witchfinders feared he might derail their activities, or maybe he had seen something he shouldn't but killed he was all the same."

"By one of the witchfinders?" asked Tranmer.

"No, Inspector. Mouser points suspicion at someone called Edward Parsley whom he took a particular dislike to. The archives show that there was such a person in the witchfinders' retinue, so perhaps he was the person who dealt with the seamier sides of the group's activities. I would propose that Parsley killed Minister Geffrey, perhaps the previous evening, and then kept his body secreted somewhere. Wherever the body was kept, it must have been fairly confined and that caused his arm to stiffen in a most unlikely way when *rigor mortis* set in."

Mrs Pilbeam said, from behind a hand that - in her shock - now covered her mouth, "How utterly gruesome. And Elizabeth Albrey, what happened to her?"

"According to Mr Houghton-Gale, she admitted to being a witch, but that is no surprise. The witchfinders had several people known as searchers, who would have kept her awake and made her constantly walk about until she would have become quite demented. It was a common practice to force people to eventually confess that they were actively involved in witchcraft."

"How barbaric. To think that it all took place in my very own parish."

"Quite so. I also learned that they may have pricked her using bodkins."

"A bodkin? Like one of my threading needles?"

"Yes, exactly the same. But these were like stage knives, retracting the needle into the handle of the bodkin so that they could claim that, when they pricked her, she felt no pain. Those areas were said to be where an imp would suckle her. So, once she confessed, the poor woman was sent to Colchester Prison and died before she could be tried."

Mr Pilbeam refilled everyone's glasses. "And so a witch from Cromwell's time and a witchfinder from our time set you off? So what about the murder of Martha Ludbrook, the once lovely Adina? Tell us about that."

"Ah, but as I do so you must remember all that I have just told you. To understand what happened in our present demands that you fully comprehend our past."

24

Rendering Invisible

"It was all too coincidental. That was why I needed to talk to someone who had knowledge about such events and you, Mr Pilbeam, kindly put me in contact with The Reverend Houghton-Gale."

"Which I would never have suggested if I'd known quite what a bounder he'd become."

"A most intriguing, if repellant, man. There was a predatory side to his manner that I was particularly averse to, but I do thank him for recommending that the archives in Chelmsford would help me understand something of the people involved. It was there that I found a file about John Stearne, one of the two principal witchfinders Henry Mouser referred to. The other one, by the way, was Matthew Hopkins, who lived in a small village very near Manningtree. According to a letter that was in Stearne's file to his mother-in-law, Hopkins had been looking after the wages they'd received for the conviction of several witches in Stowmarket. And that was the point that Kenton became the fulcrum on which all the other events have turned."

Inspector Tranmer cut in, "You see, for whatever reason, Hopkins buried the money in Leucock Plantation, during the time the group were in Kenton. But he only told Stearne where the money was. Stearne's letter alludes to this because he asks his Mother-in-law for a loan, using the buried money as surety."

Mrs Pilbeam took her large hat from beside her chair and began to fan herself. "This is all very interesting. So this witchfinder, what was his name?"

"Hopkins, my dearest."

"This Hopkins only tells Stearne where the money is hidden. But what I don't understand is why it was still there. After all, it has only just been found still buried in Leucock Plantation."

Miss Smy sipped from her glass and continued, "That was the most fascinating thing of all. You see, when I went to the archive, the letter to Mrs Cawston, Stearne's Mother-in-Law, says that he knows where the money is hidden. The instructions where to find it are quite explicit and at first I was happy to leave it at that. But then Doctor Thurston Hessett tells me that I was the fourth person to ask for the file and that three others had called to see it: Mr Pallant, Nigel Manners and Mr Houghton-Gale."

"A very popular file, Miss Smy. Sandwich anyone?" Pilbeam, having dispensed the drinks, was now passing around clean plates.

"A popular file indeed. And then I asked myself the same question that Pallant and Houghton-Gale had asked Doctor Thurston Hessett: was there a file for Stearne's mother-in-law,

Margaret Cawston? After all, her family were of some note and they did indeed have documents archived for her. That was most fascinating."

Agatha Pilbeam leaned forward enthusiastically, extolling Miss Smy with a cheery, "Do tell! I have to know!"

"In Mrs Cawston's file was a later letter from Stearne to her, pleading in the most appalling way, telling her that he had reached the place where the money was hidden, only to find it had gone missing. Stearne reassures his Mother-in-law that he is convinced it is a plot by Hopkins to deceive him and that Hopkins has buried the money elsewhere within the plantation. He's rather desperate by this time and the letter is very disjointed, almost as if Stearne is slowly losing his mind."

Pilbeam raised an arm like an inquisitive child, "I'm lost, Miss Smy. Surely the money was no great amount. Why were Pallant and Houghton-Gale so obsessed with it? So obsessed that some poor woman was murdered for it."

"Because, in his first letter to Mrs Cawston, Stearne reveals that the coins they have been paid in are no ordinary coins. They were paid with Thomas Rawlins' Oxford Crown coins, extremely rare and very valuable."

"Who's Thomas Rawlins?"

"Oh, Rawlins was Oxford's 'Graver of Seals, Stamps and Medals', and he created the coinage to honour the presence of Charles I who was staying in Oxford at the time. I can only imagine that the good burghers of Stowmarket, who were known to be staunch Parliamentarians, were glad to be rid of them."

"How much is each coin worth?" asked Mr Pilbeam.

It was Tranmer who answered. "Each coin is worth about £700.00. As they were paid £23 for their efforts, the haul has been valued at about £16,000."

Mr Pilbeam's mouth fell open, "£16,000 pounds. Why that's a very large fortune. I could very happily live on a treasure trove like that."

"Indeed," said Miss Smy. "And that was why Pallant and Houghton-Gale wanted to find them so badly. Pallant was a clever man. He was born in the same village as John Stearne and, just out of curiosity, had been doing some research on a neighbouring cottage. As soon as he'd discovered that local rumour said the cottage had once belonged to a famous witchfinder, he looked into the matter with greater interest and discovered the Stearne files in the archives at Chelmsford. Realising that a small fortune lay hidden still in one of the three plantations, he bought them at a high price. What he hadn't realised was that Houghton-Gale was also very interested and not so very far behind him."

"Miss Smy," asked Agatha Pilbeam. "How did Houghton-Gale become aware about the coins?"

"Your husband set him off."

"My husband? How come?"

"Because he sent Mouser's letter to Houghton-Gale to verify its authenticity. I believe that was what he told you, Inspector?"

"He certainly did. When Houghton-Gale read about the witchfinders, he was fascinated to know more, but the archive only has Stearne's records. Nothing exists for Hopkins. Of course, once he read about a buried hoard, and the special coins that Hopkins and Stearne had been paid with, then that became his obsession."

Miss Smy placed her sandwich, largely untouched, back on to the table. "Unfortunately for Martha Ludbrook, it did become his obsession. Hessett probably told Houghton-Gale, just like he'd told me, that there was another party interested. As soon as Houghton-Gale had found out that that other party was a certain Cecil Pallant, a magician with a very attractive assistant called Adina, he connived to get to the coins first."

The Inspector brushed some breadcrumbs from his lap before taking up the story. "What Mrs Cupper and Nigel Manners saw from their train that day was Houghton-Gale dressed as a witchfinder, with Martha Ludbrook pretending to be a hanging corpse. It had the very effect he wanted, to focus all enquiries on to Low Plantation and especially on to its new owner, Cecil Pallant."

"Misdirection!" said the Reverend Pilbeam. "So that's why you were asking your questions in the church that day. It wasn't the magician who was misdirecting the attention of the police, but Mr Houghton-Gale. Everyone's focus switched entirely on to Pallant, which would leave Houghton-Gale plenty of time to search for those coins in Leucock's Plantation. Genius!"

Inspector Tranmer shook his head. "Not so, not so. Poor Martha was caught in between and Pallant soon dragged from her what was going on. His revenge was to have her murdered in the presence of Houghton-Gale, so that the shame of his being involved with another woman - and one that had been so brutally slain - would send him scurrying back to Layer de la Haye to avoid any connection with the scandal."

"So on the night of the murder, he'd already found out that they were meeting?" asked Agatha Pilbeam. "But why did he do such a dreadful thing in such a busy road like Great Colman Street? He could have killed poor Martha at any time."

"That very question rather perplexed me," replied Miss Smy. "But then I realised that, in that one awful event, he would have achieved three things: first to be rid of someone he was close to who was betraying him; second, as the Inspector said, to get Houghton-Gale firmly out of the way."

The Pilbeams' cat appeared from the nearby bushes and walked haughtily into the group before springing on to the vicar's wife's lap.

"Ah, Bubbles!" said Mrs Pilbeam. "You're come to join us."

"Your third reason, Miss Smy?" said the Reverend, slightly irritated that the conversation had been interrupted at such an important juncture. "You said there were three reasons for Martha Ludbrook being murdered in a crowded place."

"Oh yes, the third reason was that he needed to also dispose of the spider who sat at the centre of the web: namely Thurston Hessett. After all, once the story of the murder had become public, and Houghton-Gale had probably by then been exposed by Martha's friends with whom she had shared the liaison, Hessett would have become curious. My conviction, and I'm certain it was also that of Cecil Pallant's, would be that he would have started to interrogate the same files everyone connected to this matter had been interested in. It wouldn't be long before a man of Thurston Hessett's intellect would have started to raise some rather awkward questions."

Mr Pilbeam shook his head, "It's all rather astonishing. Yes, indeed it is."

"You also have to remember that Pallant was a showman through and through," added Tranmer. "The whole illusion rested on the fact that the police would eventually deduce that it could only have been Thurston Hessett who had committed the crime. Pallant needed witnesses to point first at himself, hence why he made sure that the killer was wearing the conventional clothes of a magician, yet leave other convenient scraps of evidence that would eventually switch the focus of the investigation to poor Doctor Hessett."

"This time it was Pallant's turn to misdirect attention. It was a high-stakes strategy, but it almost worked," said Miss Smy.

"Ah," nodded Mr Pilbeam. "That was where your little visit to Ipswich Gaol saved the day."

"It was a trifling thing, but deeply important nonetheless. I must admit that I couldn't believe Hessett to be, of all things, a cold-blooded murderer, but I could quite believe such a thing of Cecil Pallant. All I needed was some small indication that would prove my intuition to be right."

"Miss Smy, who is being too modest as usual, knew that the killer had stabbed Martha from behind in the left side of her body, so must have been left-handed. That threw the spotlight straight back on to Pallant and, not realising that he had another witness in Leucock Plantation when he was pointing his gun at Miss Smy and Houghton-Gale, he confessed as much. Of course, what he hadn't realised was that Miss Smy had taken the liberty of having Spadger Peck and his double-barrelled shotgun hidden as a precaution."

"Yes, Spadger can hide anywhere, much to the chagrin of many of east Suffolk's gamekeepers. Knowing that he was hidden in that wood made me feel a lot less nervous."

"And it wasn't you that sent those notes to the two men to get them there at the same time? My husband tells me that you made him send those telegrams when he was in Ipswich to meet with the Bishop."

"Yes, by then I was banking on the fact that, with Thurston Hessett in prison and Pallant a free man again, he would not be able to resist such a meeting. Thankfully, the gamble paid off."

"Do you know, my love, I think I need something a bit more stimulating than another glass of rose lemonade. Anyone care to join me? I have a rather excellent Margaux, a *Château Prieuré-Lichine* to be exact, that is calling for me from the cellar. Can't you hear it?"

"But aren't we missing something," remonstrated Mrs Pilbeam. "The money, where did you find the money, Miss Smy? You found it when no one else could."

"That wasn't difficult. I simply asked myself where is the one place that no one would think to look? And that was underneath the very spot where Stearne had originally failed to find it. I can't be certain, but I think that Hopkins had first buried the coins a good way down and then made it look as if the coins had been stolen from a shallow hole just above them. That was masterly to my mind, because he fooled everyone."

"More misdirection, Miss Smy?" smiled the Reverend Pilbeam, shaking his head in disbelief at her imagination.

Miss Smy took the cotton bag she had brought with her and pulled out a large green jacketed book, opening it at a page she had bookmarked.

"I have borrowed this book from your library, Mr Pilbeam. Your wife said you wouldn't mind but I'm sure that, being most secretive about your conjuring, you might have frowned upon such a request. It is, as I know you recognise, your copy of Alfred Binet's *'Psychology of Prestidigitation'* in which he talks about 'Inattentional Blindness' or misdirection as you would have it. May I read a short paragraph?"

Pilbeam sat down again and gestured for her to carry on.

"It reads, *'When it is particularly important that certain peculiarities of a trick be not observed, even in the broad light, matters are so arranged that the attention of the spectators is drawn to another point at the decisive moment... The attention is thus distracted... rendering invisible a spectacle which is perfectly visible to all eyes.'*"

She closed the book triumphantly. "And that is what we have all been falling for, our attention as spectators was drawn to another point at the decisive moment."

Pilbeam rose once again from his chair and called back, "It will be the same wine I promised, but now I will choose the best vintage!"

25

Towards Monk Soham

"I know you have a short distance home, Miss Smy, but I was wondering if you might take the air with me? I was thinking of walking to Monk Soham to catch the sunset. Would you care to join me?"

Miss Smy thought for a moment before answering, "Why not? It is a beautiful evening and the view from the church is very lovely."

They had both left the vicarage together, their minds smoothed by excellent wine and leisurely conversation. As they turned on to the Eye Road they watched the swifts spinning, turning and falling, all before giddily rising again to gather in their lofty congress. The air was thin and secretive, softly stealing in and around them in warm slivers. Across the sway of the large fields, a dog's ceaseless barking was being borne by the wind above the sighing wheat.

"Can I ask a question, Miss Smy? Why did you not tell me about the meeting you had arranged between Pallant and Houghton-Gale? You placed yourself in an extremely dangerous situation. Although I accept that the outcome was successful, it could have turned out very differently."

"I didn't ask either you, PC Cornish, or any member of the constabulary because all of you wouldn't have allowed it to happen. You were all so confident that you had your man, you would have taken a very dim view of what I would have proposed."

"Quite true," sighed Tranmer.

"Will they hang Mr Pallant?"

"I can only give you my official answer to that."

"Something about it is not for you to give your opinion on such matters? Only the judge can decide on the severity of the sentence and so on."

"Yes, something like that. It may well be the one escape act that he isn't able to extricate himself from."

Smy folded her arms as she walked along, imbibing the intoxicating scents of wildflowers that gently quivered beneath the hedgerows.

"Perhaps we might play again together soon, Miss Smy? I very much enjoyed our Dvořák piece."

"Yes, perhaps."

"I still maintain you accompany my instrument very skilfully. Did you ever take up the violin yourself?"

"No, I never did, but I once knew someone who played the violin very beautifully. Very beautifully indeed."

"From your time in London? I'm afraid my playing would be rather too rough and ready in comparison."

Miss Smy stopped and turned towards Tranmer and looked up at his childlike face. She wondered how, with all of the ills that those eyes witnessed, he could still retain such an air of unsullied innocence. "You play very well; I have said it before. But some people have a touch that almost makes me believe in God. I knew one person..." There was a definite catch in her throat as she spoke, but she continued, "...who played so divinely that you desperately wanted to stop playing yourself, afraid that your own musical fumbling might desecrate something enormously sacred."

Tranmer found that he had nothing to say. It was as if he had chanced upon some hidden well of grief that she had been trying to keep from sight. Smy smiled momentarily and walked on. "There, now I am talking too much."

"But you must tell me all about them. I would love to know who they were."

"Some stories can be told at any time and some can never be told. Believe me, Herbert, that is a story that can never be told."

Acknowledgements

This book may have my name on the front, but there were many people who also generously contributed their advice and help and whom I would personally like to thank. So, in alphabetical first name order, I would like to express my appreciation to Andrew Marsh for everything he does as the owner of the unrivalled Dial Lane Books in Ipswich; Aude Cazenove for correcting my appalling schoolboy French; Doreen and David Matthews for their deep knowledge about Kenton and 'Suffolk ways'; Elizabeth Barrett for her historical advice and equine knowledge; Essex Record Office for the chapter on Dr Thurston Hessett's place of work; Lucy Johnson for the beautiful cover design; Penny Barkas for her tireless proofreading and insightful suggestions; Sheena Bulpitt for her wonderful cover art and Stephen Boulton for his sensitive and timely suggestion.

Melissa Nash created the excellent period map of the Kenton district to complement both this book and the first in the Winifred Smy series, *Killing Time in Kenton*. It is free to download at: https://michaelheathauthor.com/genres/murder-mystery